I0689755

SIREN
OF
STONE
By
Ruth Nalio

INDIE
BACK
PRESS

BOOK THREE

1

<u>TRIGGER WARNING:</u>
This book contains sensitive material related to:
Abduction
Violence/Death
Murder/Assassination
Strong Language
Sex
Child Abuse
Substance Abuse
Dismemberment
Blood/Gore
Mutilation of Corpse
Exhibitionism
Immolation
Imprisonment
PTSD/CPTSD
Voyeurism
Sexual Assault
Crude language
Slavery
Sexism
Bigotry
Homophobia
Hunting
Illegal Activities
Destruction
Genocide
Self-Mutilation
Bondage
3

Dedication

This book is dedicated to all the boss-ass women out there, all my cold-blooded ladies who don't need no damn man. This book is also dedicated to all the men who respect a woman and like to do just what lil' mamma says like a good boy.

*Authors Note: This prologue is a very twisted and dramatized version of a personal experience—a way of facing the trauma I've endured and worked to heal from. I aged my character up, as I was only three the first time I was abused and twelve the second. **I in no way condone abuse at any age.**

Immortal World
Book 3: Siren of Stone
Prologue

Alla or Ella for short...

The King had told me I would be amusing. At first, I hadn't understood what he meant. For four long years, I remained ignorant of his true intentions. The first four years of my captivity were filled with brutal training. My aggressors were always grown men, ordered not to hold back—only to preserve my life. Every day, I was pushed harder, taught to fight, to survive. The King had promised me that I would fight in the gladiator pits one day, that he would return for me when I was old enough.

I spent those years preparing, training in hand-to-hand combat, learning how to kill with my bare hands. The King's eyes were always watching from a distance, never intervening—his presence always felt, even when his hands weren't on me. His words echoed in my ears: "You will be mine to watch when you're ready. When you are, you will amuse me more than any other."

5

My first night in the care of the King was a grim precursor to the next six years of my life. He watched as his servants washed me and locked me in a pillory, knowing he'd honed me into a weapon for the last four years. Then he approached, looking me over with a curious expression.

"Tell me, where do you come from?" he asked, his voice carrying a faint note of curiosity.

Ignoring the chafing of the wood around my neck and wrists, I let my anger rise. "An island where males go to die at the hands of starving females," I spat, though the pressure of the pillory against my throat made my words sound weaker than I intended. Had my mother known this would happen to us?

"Ah, yes, the 'Siren' tale. If you are indeed a Siren, why are you the one on your knees, locked so helplessly in that pillory?"

"My sisters and I have yet to come into our powers," I replied, forcing down my fear. "But when we do, you'll regret this day."

"So, if you come from an island of all women, have you ever been with a man? Or are you still innocent to the pleasures of the flesh, I wonder?" He circled me, his eyes lingering. "When I asked my wife about her slave, her little golden pet, she said she was a meek girl. In fact it took her days to calm down and she was easily made to heel. You're not like that, though, are you?"

"Mother said I was born with my father's fire inside me," I answered, starved for any news of my sisters but unwilling to show that weakness, "while Kassandra has always been a delicate island flower." I would never admit that males unsettled me.

6

He chuckled, an unsettling sound. "Now then, Siren," the King said, grabbing my hips with a bruising grip, "let's see what kind of fight you put up in this position."

He lifted my dress and forced himself into me. Pain tore through me as I cried out, my insides searing from the intrusion. I'd seen my mother and aunts take males in pleasure—how had they endured it? There was no pleasure here, only agony. He released himself inside me repeatedly, striking and biting my body as I screamed for him to stop. When he left the room, it wasn't over. He returned with others and watched as they brutalized me until dawn.

The King had kept me in his pillory only a few weeks before tossing me to the gladiators. He'd started with one at first, and as my ability to resist them had grown, he'd increased the number of opponents. My rape had gone from taking place in a cell to being held in a public arena with a roaring crowd, a crowd that was always most excited when the gladiators pinned me down and used my broken and bloody body for their own pleasures.

A decade later, I was shoved into the arena dressed in sheer fabric, armed only with a crude bludgeon. The King demanded entertainment, and I was it. Once, I'd asked what he would do if I refused to fight, and he'd shown me my sisters—Amaltheia working for one of the soldiers that had captured us, and Kassandra working for the Queen, wearing soft cotton, doing her hair with the other serving girls. He'd told me that should I refuse to fight; he would toss them to the gladiators and soldiers to do with as they pleased. So, I fought.

7

Ares, our father, visited me once. I had never known what he looked like, only that he was Ares, the God of War. He appeared outside my cell, disguised as a guard, his imposing form framed by the dim light of the corridor. Through the iron bars, he studied me, tilting his head with a curiosity I hadn't seen in the others.

"What do you want?" I asked, wary of his presence.

"You've piqued my interest," he said, his voice cool, "with your fighting—and because I am your father."

For a fleeting moment, hope ignited within me, fragile yet bright. "Have you come to take us away from this place?" I asked, my voice trembling with the daring belief that rescue might finally be within reach.

He laughed—a cold, dismissive sound that shattered my hope. "Rescue?" he said, his tone mocking. "You are unworthy of rescue if you cannot save yourself."

Without another word, he vanished, leaving me alone to rot in my stifling, rancid cell.

I remembered that visit from him that day as I stumbled into the arena, the crowd's roar vibrating through my bones. Straightening my back, I walked forward and spotted a shield. I knew it wouldn't be a fair fight and could never win, but that didn't mean I would go down easily. I wanted these males to hurt. Some of my adversaries had died, and others had been left unable to claim the reward of my battered body at the end of the fight. It wasn't our prick of a father who hardened my spine—it was this.

As the gladiators' gates opened, I charged forward, rolling to snatch the shield as I moved. They rushed at me, but I twisted away at the last moment, swinging my pathetic club into the shin

8

of one of them. He toppled with a grunt. Swiveling in the sand, I brought the shield down on his exposed neck. The sensation of the metal pulling through flesh brought back the memory of the last time he and his companions had violated my body, and I laughed.

Twisting around, I charged at another gladiator, only to drop and skid across the dirt below his reach. I came up between his legs with my club, striking with such force that he flipped forward and landed on his face.

My satisfaction was short-lived as a blow connected with my ribs, driving the air from my lungs. I fell forward but twisted and kicked out blindly, my foot connecting somewhere on my attacker's legs. As he toppled, a fist locked into my hair, yanking me back through the sandy dirt. He stepped over me, trying to pin me, but I swung the club into the side of his knee, feeling and hearing the crunch of both the club and his joint. He cried out in pain, his hands flying to the wound. Dropping my weapon, I laced my fingers together and brought my fists into his side, sending him sprawling off me.

Another male charged. Rolling through the sand, I shoved myself upright and ran toward the arena wall. I climbed a few steps up the wall and twisted mid-air, landing a kick to his face that sent him sprawling on the ground. The crowd's roar, which had once terrified me, was now nothing more than noise. All I heard—all I focused on—was the pounding of my heart.

Looking at the remaining men, I felt a strange, uncontrollable cry building in my throat. As I charged forward, the itch in my throat erupted into a deafening battle cry. The men

9

rushing at me stumbled, dropping their weapons as they tripped over themselves.

I almost did the same when I saw them fall to their knees. Breathing heavily, I scanned the three remaining gladiators. One was barely holding himself upright on a shattered knee. I looked up at the oddly silent crowd and saw that the females were the only ones unaffected. Their eyes were fixed on me.

Turning, I glanced at the unconscious male behind me and saw his jaw hanging unnaturally, nearly detached from his face. It had happened, and the moment my mother had long given up on had finally arrived.

I walked forward, gripping the nearest gladiator's face between my hands. His adoring eyes gazed up at me as I easily snapped his neck. Feminine screams filled the air as I smiled—a cold, humorless smile fueled by the new strength coursing through my body.

Atlantis would fall. I would free my sisters. Then we would find Ares and kill him.

Chapter 1

During a heated fight in the middle of a hunt, Ella throws a punch at Kassie, knocking her into the water. As Kassie splashes beneath the surface and Ella turns back to Theia to continue fighting, a swarm of gators erupts from the depths. Their powerful jaws snap dangerously close, dragging Kassie under while keeping Ella and Theia at bay...
Ella...

Bigfoot surged out of the water with Kassie's blood and muck-covered body draped over his shoulder. He glanced over his shoulder as the gators climbed the bank, snapping at his heels.

"Go!" I yelled again, the sight of my sister's unmoving form sending a jolt of fear through me that I hadn't felt in twelve thousand years. The hair-covered monster turned and disappeared into the swamp within moments. As he vanished, I focused on Theia. "I'm coming, Theia!" I yelled as I bashed in the head of the gator that had been keeping me from Kassie.

"Just get yourself up a damn tree!" she yelled, yanking her stick out of the gator's eye. The massive reptile shook its head, pawing at its face. Theia threw herself forward and stabbed the stick into the other eye before the creature could escape. The

11

gator bucked, its massive tail lifting it off the ground, 800 pounds of scaly muscle beneath my delicately framed sister. She grabbed the stick she'd jammed into the eye and pushed it even further into the socket until the gator stopped thrashing and went still beneath her. With strength and speed no mortal would have been capable of, she pulled the bloodied stick from its socket, pushed to her feet, and dashed for the dropped gun. A beautiful spin on her heel, the echoing sound of a shotgun blast, and the new gator coming for her jerked and then fell still in death.

The remaining gators slipped back into the water, and Theia made her way to where I stood, braced against a tree, a gator dead at my blood-soaked feet.

"You sent our sister away with Bigfoot!" she yelled at me.

"I sent our sister to safety! What was I supposed to do? She would be dead right now if he hadn't saved her!" I shot back.

"I was working on it!" she snapped, tears streaking her filthy face.

I closed my eyes. "I wasn't going to take that chance." I opened my eyes and looked at her. "We need to get home where I can heal. Then we will head back out and look for her."

"Ella, what if he finishes her off?" Theia's question was quiet as she slipped her arm around my waist, acting as a human crutch. I felt angry that I even needed her help, but I knew we needed to move quickly.

"He could have killed us several times over. I think he feels the need to protect us for some reason," I told her, hoping I was right. My sisters thought I was fearless, but in reality, I was terrified—terrified of living without them and terrified of dying

12

and finding myself in the hell that had been the ten years spent at the mercy of the gladiators and the king.

"I hope you're right," she said as we headed back through the swamp toward the fanboat. "What are we going to tell the boatman?"

"That the gators dragged her under. We don't need to tell him that Bigfoot took her—he'd never believe us. Not to mention, I've got the gator bite to prove we ran into trouble. If he asks questions, we can just shake our heads and act distraught."

Theia snorted. "Do you even know how to act distraught?"

"I'm in shock, then." I glared at her. The flesh on my calf had been shredded by the gator that had attacked me. "Just look at my damn leg that would toss a human into shock. Pathetic." I'd been so weak as a human without my immortality, but I'd still survived worse than this.

"Where do you think he'll take her?" Theia switched back to Kassie and Bigfoot without transition.

"Somewhere safe for her to heal and hopefully close to home," I muttered. The first time we'd encountered him had been near our own home. Theia and I fell silent as we returned to the fanboat. When we finally made it back, the boat was empty. I frowned and looked around.

"Clay!" Theia called out, helping me the rest of the way to the boat. "Clay! Where are you?" She yelled into the surrounding swamp. "He's always here," she muttered. "Clay!" She called again, her voice laced with forced desperation.

"Theia, isn't it strange that Bigfoot found us today when we've been going out of our way to find a faraway place to

13

hunt?" I asked as I pulled his book from under his seat and saw that it was the same one he'd been reading the first day, the bookmark still in place.

"Maybe he's following us?" She replied calmly before calling for Clay again with a distraught voice.

"Isn't this the same book he was reading the first day we hired him?"

"Really? Kassie's boyfriend is missing; we're supposed to be faking her death because she's been rescued by an overgrown apeman, and you're worried about what book he's reading?"

Looking over the boat's edge, I noted the footprints—massive, shoeless footprints. My head swiveled back to look around the inside of the boat again. "Clay's shoes and the rest of his clothes are in the boat."

"What?" Theia leaned over and looked at the discarded clothing. "So he's running around the swamp naked?"

"With our sister over his shoulder," I confirmed, pointing at the tracks.

Theia's head swiveled back around, and she walked over to the footprints, crouching down. "Holy fuck. Clay is the Apeman!"

"When I heal, I'm going to kill him," I said coldly. He'd been tricking us for weeks! What had he been planning? How had he planned it?

"Fuck!" Theia turned and looked at me. "We all sang to him that first day, remember? Kassie called him in instead of the coypu!"

I closed my eyes and muttered, "Damn it." My eyes snapped open, confusion clouded my gaze as I looked at her. "It

14

doesn't make any sense, though. He hasn't been acting like someone under the spell. He even challenged me in his Sasquatch form. Do you think he's only entrapped by Kassie? We've never really tried to entrap one male to all three of us." Not that we used our power to entrap males that often in the first place.

Theia shrugged helplessly. "Do you think she's still in danger? I mean, if he is enslaved to her, then he'll want only to satisfy her every desire, following her every command."

"We can only hope that she's safe with him. We'll wait here for an hour, then go home. He may have taken her there. If not, we can get his address from the dock office and get her."

Theia sighed and climbed onto the boat. "He may bring her back to the boat, but we both know that's not going to happen." She stepped around me, opened Clay's cooler, and got out a bottle of water before crouching in front of me. "Let's get you cleaned up." She handed me the bottle before taking hold of my boot. She looked up at me. "Ready?"

"Aren't I always?" I asked, leaning back in the seat to brace myself. Pain was part of my everyday existence; it was the one thing that kept my Siren abilities under control and my Demons at bay. Theia pulled my boot from my foot as carefully as she could, the fabric of my jeans shredded and embedded into the boot and my flesh. Pain seared sharply through my leg as she removed it. Next, she ripped my pant leg up to my knee, the feel of the fabric being pulled out of my skin both painful and sickening. Theia tied my shredded pants just above my knee before taking the water bottle and rinsing my wound.

"It looks like there might be a tooth in here. Let me rinse my knife, and I'll get it out for you." Theia pulled out her pocket

15

knife and rinsed it with the water. We'd learned a long time ago that leaving things in our wounds meant healing over them and then having to cut them out, so it was best to get it out before you healed.

I pulled my lighter from my pocket and handed it to her. "For the knife."

She took the lighter and ran the blade through the flame to further sterilize it. "Brace." That one word was all the warning she gave before pushing the tip of the knife into my leg and pressing it against the side of the tooth. She used the knife and her finger to pull the tooth from my leg, blood flowing from the inch-deep hole as I gritted my teeth against the pain. "Looks like there's some real muscle damage here. You won't be fully healed for a couple of days."

"I'll be ready to go by morning," I told her bluntly.

"I didn't say you wouldn't be, just that you won't be fully healed. I know you'll push through this shit and make it worse, but that's because you're a fucking masochist."

"Aren't we all?" I asked honestly. My sisters never understood it when I tossed this saying at them, but the truth was, we were all continuing to live with our pain—pain from twelve thousand years of memories. Twelve thousand years of watching whole civilizations rise and fall, of watching females and children suffer and die for no reason. Twelve thousand years of having only each other to keep us going and sane. "Let's get going. I don't feel like waiting around for nothing. You and I both know he's not bringing her back to the boat, or he would have been here before us."

16

Chapter 2

Ella...

Theia and I made it back to the manor. She helped me out of the boat before I shoved her off and limped toward the house. My pride wouldn't let her assist me. It was something the three of us had in common. Our time in Atlantis had hardened us against taking help when we were injured. I'd been doctored just enough to keep me alive in the cells and left to heal—and suffer—in darkness over and over for an entire decade. Kassie never spoke of her pain, but she bore a single scar on her back, one that told me she'd been whipped at least once. Her refusal to accept help hinted at more suffering than she let on. Now Kassie was left with Bigfoot as she healed.

Blood ran down my leg as I forced myself to walk to the porch. Stopping, I collapsed into the chair and glared at my injury. "You'll need to grab some bandages. I'm not in the mood to clean blood off the floors. Either that, or I'll sleep out here." There was a knife in my pocket that would get the job done.

Theia crossed her arms and cocked a brow. "Why would I bother bandaging you up? You're just going to bleed out in the shower anyway. I'll clean it up—I'm a mess, too." She held out

17

her hand to me. "And before you say no, the sooner you shower, the sooner I can patch myself up. Dried blood sucks ass."

"Ain't that the truth." I grudgingly took her hand and let her wrap an arm around my waist.

"I'm still pissed that he took her, and you just let him," she said as she helped me through the door.

"Would you rather she'd been eaten alive? At least now we know Bigfoot is Clay, and we stand a chance of finding her."

"This is the first time we've been separated in over twelve thousand years. I don't like it."

"Opinions are like assholes, Theia, and right now you're showing yours." She suddenly let go of my waist, causing me to fall. "What the hell!"

She crossed her arms and glared at me. "Have fun with the steps. I'm going to clean myself up." With that, she walked away.

A roar of frustration escaped me. If not for my injuries, I would have attacked her without hesitation. Theia and I had always fought. Even before Atlantis, we bickered, shoved, and hit each other. Atlantis only amplified our violent tendencies. Kassie, on the other hand, was mild—obedient. She'd always tried to calm us when we fought.

I rubbed my face and struggled to my feet, using the wall for support. Theia was scowling and waiting at the top when I reached the top of the staircase. "I thought you were cleaning up?" I snapped.

Her jaw twitched, and she turned to look away from me. "I shouldn't have dropped you, Kassie would be pissed."

"She'd call you a shitty ass crutch." I gritted out as I struggled with my fifth step. This was bullshit! Theia sighed

18

heavily before coming down to help me. "Back off," I growled. "I don't need your help."

"You can kick my ass for it when you heal, but I'm helping you up the steps the rest of the damn way, okay bitch?"

"Go suck a dick."

"Shove it and eat taint," Theia shot back, wrapping her arm around my waist despite my smacking her hand away.

"Such an insult coming from a two-way light switch," I muttered bitterly.

"Sometimes pussy just doesn't scratch the itch, and unlike you, I'm not into self-mutilation."

"Right, you just piss me off instead," I replied. What she didn't know was that being beaten until I'd lost consciousness was the only thing that spared me from remembering most of my abuse back then. The times I'd been knocked out and woken to find myself bandaged and left in my cell had been my best days. The other times, I'd been held down and violated in more ways than I cared to remember.

"Whatever, twat-face," she mumbled, practically carrying me up the steps.

"How badly were you injured by those gators?" I asked, realizing I'd been too concerned with Kassie to check on my other sister.

"Just tail-whipped and clawed a bit. I'm not sure how I avoided being bitten. I wasn't thinking about anything but Kassie," she admitted.

"Same." Though relief that she was relatively unscathed flickered in me, it didn't touch my tone. Anger and indifference were my shields, even with my sisters. "You can fucking let go

19

now. I got it from here," I informed her as we reached the top of the steps.

"Whatever, twat-face," she repeated, this time clearer, as she finally let go of me.

"Take it up the ass," I shot back, using the wall for support to help myself to my room. The pain wasn't the issue; it was the goddamned useless muscle that had been damaged. Stumbling like a fucking invalid, I slammed my door shut behind me and limped to the bathroom.

Usually, I'd strip before getting in the shower, but my clothes were already fucked, so I kept them on as I climbed into the tub. Reaching into the soap basket, I picked up the knife I kept there and drew it hard and deep across my throat, severing my vocal cords. Hot blood ran down my chest as I gargled and choked on the thick metallic substance. In seconds, the light was replaced by blackness as I slipped out of consciousness. This time, there were no dreams—only a deathless void, a fleeting reprieve from the torment of my eternal existence.

***

Ella...

It was still dark outside when I woke, probably around four or five in the morning, knowing how my healing worked. While my calf was still sore and the skin still pink, my throat held nearly no pain. The few times Kassie or Theia had ended up with their throats slit, they had experienced more rapid healing of the wound. I figured it had something to do with our vocal cords being our primary power source. Pushing to my feet in the shower-tub combo, I shut the curtain before turning on the water.

20

I didn't give a fuck what temperature the water was; I just needed to get the dried blood off.

As the water sprayed, I peeled my ruined clothing from my body and left it lying at my feet. Grabbing my shampoo, I scrubbed it into my hair without moving out from under the increasingly hot spray of the shower. The water running off my body had a reddish brown tint, washing the blood and dirt down the drain from last night. Grabbing my conditioner, I repeated the process of scrubbing it through my now filth-free hair. Next, I grabbed my loofah and lathered it with the exfoliating body wash I kept in the shower. When you were scrubbing dried blood off your body every day, you used abrasives on your skin. Being a fucking Siren meant that my skin stayed soft and didn't get dried from over-exfoliating, not that I gave a flying fuck; it was just nice not to itch all the time.

Turning the water off, I threw back the curtain, grabbed the towel hanging on the holder, and stepped out, wrapping it around myself. My damned calf burnt like a mother fucker; good. The pain helped keep the itch at bay. Physical pain kept the emotional scars pushed back as well. Theia called me a masochist, and she was right. The pain was my release from all the Demons in my mind. Walking out of the bathroom and into my bedroom, I dropped the towel on the floor and opened my dresser, pulling out jeans, socks, underwear, sports bra, and a shirt. My shit stayed stacked, an entire outfit always at the ready.

Once dressed, I walked out of my room and down to the kitchen to make coffee. Theia wouldn't be up for at least an hour. We would figure out what to do from there about Kassie. It was possible that Clay wouldn't bring her back until she regained

21

consciousness. It was also possible that he wouldn't bring her home at all. Fucking Sasquatch. Pain burned and pinched in my calf with each step down to the first floor, making me more irritable. Self-inflicted pain was a good pain, but pain caused by someone else just pissed me off. I was in control of my body, in control of what I did and didn't feel.

As I reached the main floor, the rich, earthy aroma of brewing coffee mingled with the soft gurgle of the coffee maker, a comforting yet surprising welcome to the morning's tension. "You're up early," I said as Theia stepped into the kitchen doorway.

"A seven-foot swamp monster has our sister," Theia replied bitterly, "did you expect me to sleep well?"

"I thought you'd sleep at least another hour," I admitted as I walked into the kitchen to sit at the table and wait for enough coffee to fill my cup.

"Well, I didn't. So, what's the plan? Are we heading out after coffee, or what?" She demanded, leaning against the counter with her arms crossed.

"How long do you think Kassie will be unconscious?" I asked instead.

"You think that liar is just waiting for her to wake up before bringing her back? He's been pulling the wool over our eyes for weeks!" Theia snapped.

"I'm not denying that Sasquatch needs to be taught a lesson, but the fuck has had plenty of chances to kill us and hasn't. He even killed those Grunch bastards that night, prick." Just another reason for me to be pissed at him.

22

Theia rolled her eyes. "Forget that he stole your fun that night. Do you think he's really keeping her safe, or do you think this has all been some sort of elaborate trick to separate us and take us out one by one?"

"Did you see what he did to that tree?" I asked with an arched brow. While I wanted the fucker dead, I wasn't delusional. Our biggest strength was intelligence. "If he wanted us dead, we'd be dead."

"Right, he didn't need to separate us, he's fucking powerful." She said, chewing her lip ring.

"Pour me some coffee," I said as I mulled over our options. "Bigfoot is as much a mystery to the immortal community as it is to the human one. Maybe that's why Clay didn't tell us. Or maybe Kassie did entrap him somehow, I don't know."

Theia walked over with my cup and sat it in front of me before going back to doctor her own with milk and sugar. "So do we go out looking for her?" She asked with her back to me, tension lining her slender shoulders.

"Let's stick close to home for now, in case he's just waiting for her to wake up or something." And because I couldn't move well enough to be of any use should shit go sideways, but I didn't admit to that.

"I doubt that. I just feel like there is something more to this." Theia sat in the chair across from me, her coffee in hand.

"I didn't say we weren't looking for her today, just that we would stay close to home. If we don't find her by this afternoon, we can go to the dock in town and get his address."

23

"Because the Swamp Ape would keep his home address on file there?" Sarcasm saturated her words.

"Do you have a better idea?" I asked, taking a drink of my coffee and looking at her expectantly.

"Whatever." We fell silent as we drank our coffee. After her first cup, Theia got up and started making eggs while drinking her second.

I understood her frustration, but I also knew there was little we could do. Had Bigfoot not shown up, Kassie may have very well died. He'd hesitated before leaving as though he were thinking of saving us all. Thinking back to the night of the Grunch, I realized that he would have been able to slaughter every last gator yesterday. Had I made the wrong call in my fear for my sister? In twelve-thousand years, I'd never second-guessed myself. This was the first time since leaving Atlantis that we'd been separated. Even when I caused the fall of Troy, we'd been together, reveling in the bloodshed together.

The tiniest twinge of pain tugged at my heart. Helen had been the only female I'd ever loved. Menelaus probably wouldn't have gone after her if it hadn't been for me. While she was as beautiful as legends claimed, Menelaus had been easily swayed by a single hum from me. I hadn't entrapped him, only convinced him that he loved another more. Had Helen not begged me to spare the father of her children, I would have killed him.

Helen had convinced me to let her play her part as his wife by day, but away from the eyes of others, she was mine. She'd tasted of the sweetest honey; her skin was soft and warm, her touch gentle and kind. All things I'd never experienced in Atlantis. While my time in Atlantis had been pain, darkness, and

24

carnage, Helen had been sunshine and laughter. Then Paris came along, bringing an end to the last remnants of softness left inside me.

The coffee mug shattered in my hand, jolting me out of my memories.

"Shit, Ella! What the hell?" Theia exclaimed, jumping at the stove.

Pushing to my feet, I didn't answer her; I just grabbed a towel and began cleaning up my mess. "Let's go look for Kassie after we eat. I'm not sitting around on my ass all damn morning." I said before limping out of the kitchen.

"Ella!" Theia yelled at me, moving the skillet of eggs to another burner and flicking off the stove.

"What?" I asked in a bored tone, turning to face her.

"What was that about? Are you okay?" Concern was etched on her beautiful face.

"Troy," I said simply.

"Right. I should have known. The eggs are done, by the way. You want some toast, too?" She knew better than to pry or comment, not unless she wanted to piss me off.

"Whatever. I just need food to keep going."

She rolled her eyes. "Why do I even bother?" Turning away, she walked back into the kitchen. I hobbled out to the front porch, grabbing my machete and sharpener on the way. Sitting on the steps, I began the rhythmic process of sharpening my blade. Each pass over the steel became a life I'd taken that day, a male I'd killed as I carved my way into the city.

I'd sung and entrapped every man within earshot, commanding them to fight without mercy. The bloodshed had

25

been magnificent, especially knowing how much Helen had despised violence. The sand had turned red with blood, the seafoam tinted pink as it lapped at the carnage. It wasn't until after Helen's death that I learned Aphrodite had played a role in her abandonment of me—at the command of my father.

Theia came outside and set a plate next to me. The toast was smothered with eggs and cheese. "We will eventually find him and make him pay for what happened," she said softly. I knew she meant our father. We'd tried for centuries to find him and kill him. Every time we inched toward happiness, he interfered, stoking the rage of others around us. Ares, God of War, had manipulated his daughters for centuries without our realization. He'd led us to incite battle after battle, war after war. Only later did we discover his hand in it all.

"It doesn't matter. She's long dead," I said as I picked up my plate and began eating. Helen had taken in my blood-covered appearance in horror that day. She'd sworn to never forgive me. I'd been so full of hate and hurt over her betrayal that I didn't want her back. Instead, I let her live and be taken back by Menelaus to live with that image of me for the rest of her days.

Chapter 3

Ella...

After eating and finishing our coffee, Theia and I went out in the direction we'd been hunting when we'd first encountered BigFoot. It was the best place to start. As much as I wanted to find them and be done with it, I knew this course of action was a lost cause. Pain sizzled through my calf with every sinking, sucking step I took in the swamp. Each pain-filled step left me wondering how bad off Kassie was. She'd been unconscious and covered in blood.

Despite my violent nature and bloodlust, I hated seeing my sisters injured. Kassie was the delicate, sweet one—the most normal of the three of us. Her distaste for males seemed to stem from constantly losing them in some terrible way. Now, her most recent romantic interest had turned out to be a huge, hairy beast with unimaginable strength. If I were being honest, I didn't think I could win a one-on-one fight against him, even with the element of surprise. And to be brutally honest, I wasn't sure I could do that to Kassie.

"Ella, this is bullshit. We're just getting filthy and exhausted when you should be recovering."

27

"Fuck off, poll-buffer. I'm fine." I snapped.

"For crying out loud! I'm going home. If you want to slow us down when we actually catch up to that hairy bastard, go for it!"

I let out a roar of frustration and slung my machete into a tree. "Fuck this! I fucking hate this whole goddamned mess!"

"Finally! It's about damn time you admit that this is fucked!" Theia yelled at me.

"I didn't have a fucking choice but to send her with him unless you wanted me just to let her get eaten alive." My voice cracked as I let my anger show, the pain I usually hid slipping through.

"Good Gods! I'm not bitching that you did what you could at the moment; I'm pissed that you have been acting like this shit isn't fucked up!"

"I never said it wasn't!" I snapped, her words only stoking my irritation. Theia was pissing me off more than the fucking mud was.

"Right, because yesterday you weren't just defending that Swamp Ape," she shot back, sarcasm dripping from her voice.

"Come say that shit to my face." My tone was cold and impassive as I challenged my sister.

Theia ran her hands through her hair, letting out a frustrated growl. "This is exactly what got us into this mess! If we'd stopped bitching at each other, maybe one of us would have seen the damn gators." She leaned her back against a tree and slid into a crouch. "It's as much your fault as it is mine."

We stayed like that for a few moments, neither of us speaking. It wasn't until the sounds of the swamp grew nearly

28

deafening that I cleared my throat. "We should head back. If my leg isn't healed yet, none of her wounds are. If Clay actually cares about her safety, he wouldn't move until tomorrow."

"Assuming he intends to let her go," Theia added.

"Ass-you-me. Now get up twat-waffle, or I'm dragging you home."

"Twat-waffle? Really?" Theia asked, raising a brow.

"I'm trying to be nice. It's not my thing." My tone was bland again, my mask slipping back into place, and the simmering anger beneath it shoved down once more.

"Obviously." She rolled her eyes as she got to her feet. "Thanks for letting me wallow for a few minutes. I needed that hit to my self-esteem."

"It's like you forget who you're talking to. I enjoy pain, remember?"

"You'd love to watch the world burn, start to heal, then pick the scabs and start the fire over, I get it."

She wasn't far off. Theia knew me too well. Without responding, I turned and began trudging back to the manor. As much as I hated being still, there wasn't much I could do until late tonight or even tomorrow morning, thanks to my leg. Each step sucked my feet into the swamp I so despised. It was only a matter of time before we'd have to move again. There were few places I'd ever been happy, and that happiness had always been fleeting. The last time I'd truly felt it was in Sparta, nearly four thousand years ago. Before that? A single day—the day Atlantis sank beneath the sea forever.

Theia stayed ahead of me the whole way back, but she never got so far that I couldn't see her. By the time I reached the

29

yard, she'd already bounded up the steps and disappeared inside. I was aggravatedly climbing the porch steps when she returned, arms full of my sharpening stone and a few of my blades.

"Here, bitch face," she said, tossing them toward me. "Something to keep you occupied."

"You know me so well."

"Love you too, twat-waffle." She watched as I put the stuff down at the top of the steps before asking, "Do you think it's too early for a drink?"

"Are you worried about liver damage?" I countered.

"You make a good point. Want one?"

"Sure," I said, sitting down and picking up my things. The familiar weight of the sharpening stone in my hand was a comfort, akin to the way a warm blanket and a book were for Kassie. Spitting on the stone, I began running a blade over it. The vibration tingling through my hand and up to my elbow, the movement forming a soothing rhythm—a slow, deliberate dance for my soul. Weapons, blood, and violence were the sweet melodies of my life.

Theia returned with a beer and sat on the other end of the step across from me, staring off into the swamp. "It feels wrong not having her here."

"It *is* wrong," I corrected, not looking up. Since reuniting, the three of us had spent every night under the same roof. Even when Kassie had her lovers, she'd never stayed the whole night with any of them. When I'd been with Helen, they had always been just a few rooms away.

"Well, we'll just have to fix it tomorrow. Hell, once she wakes up, she might even have that hairy fuck scratch her itch." Theia joked bitterly.

"Do you think our sister is dark enough to scratch her itch and then rip his heart out?" The vivid image of a male lying beneath me, his chest ripped open and bloody, his heart in my hand filled my mind.

"Probably not. At least not the way you're imagining it," Theia said, glancing at me before tipping back her bottle of beer.

"How do you think I'm imagining it?" I asked, already knowing she was right before she answered.

"Bloody." She said simply.

"You'd be right."

"You're just too predictable in your lust," she stated, re-adjusting her back against the rail support.

"You mean my *blood-lust*?"

"Yeah, that."

We fell silent, drinking our beers as I continued sharpening my knives. The rhythmic motion of the blade against the stone was grounding, even as thoughts of bloodshed stirred somewhere in the back of my mind. Once her beer was gone, Theia went inside to play her games.

It wasn't long before she came back out, looking just as restless as I felt. The difference was that I kept my restlessness in check. I kept nearly *everything* in check.

"Argh! I'm going crazy!" Theia complained, punching one of the supports for the porch roof.

"You went crazy a long time ago."

31

"Fuck you, you knew what I meant." She was a bitter bitch when she was frustrated.

"Go to the barn and take the edge off, then," I said, setting my stuff down and pulling off my boot. My calf was still a little sore, but it didn't look bad. The skin was pink, still healing, but no longer a concern.

"You should be ready to go by morning, right?" Theia asked, walking over to inspect my leg for herself.

"We could go out tonight," I said, looking up at her.

"Right, but if you need to run or anything the internal damage is still there. We should probably wait until morning."

"Whatever, I'm going to go clean the shotgun." I hated that she was right.

"You mean take it apart and deep clean it," Theia said dryly.

"That's what cleaning a gun *is*." If your weapons weren't properly maintained, they would fall apart.

She sighed heavily. "It was used one time. You could probably just get away with cleaning the barrel."

"When have you known me to half-ass anything?" I countered, struggling to keep my temper in check. Theia was getting on my nerves. Being stuck at the damn manor while Kassie was missing was getting on my nerves. Hell, even the sounds of the swamp were getting on my nerves.

"I can see you're about to blow your top. I'll leave you alone," Theia said before walking down the steps and heading toward the barn.

"Bitch," I muttered under my breath, hating that I was still healing and wanting nothing more than to hit something.

32

"Your fists still work; you could throw some punches, too," Theia called over her shoulder. I wasn't sure if she'd heard me call her a bitch or if she just knew how I was feeling.

Pulling my boot back on, I got to my feet and made my way down the steps. My calf was still sore as fuck, but at least it wasn't the searing pain it had been earlier today. By the time I reached the barn, I was almost walking normally. Covering up my pain was something I was better at than either of my sisters.

Theia was waiting for me just inside where she greeted me with pretty words. "I'll hold the bag for you if you hold it for me first."

"Good. Gives me a chance to tell you what's wrong with your form. You've been getting sloppy," I told her honestly as I moved toward the punching bag. Pretty words weren't my style.

"You're such a bitch."

"You love me anyway," I said, my tone flat and humorless.

"Glad to see you're lightening up a little. I was worried you'd be in a bad mood the rest of the day."

Theia and I spent the next few hours in the barn before heading inside for the night. Dinner consisted of leftovers we didn't bother to heat properly. Afterward, Theia took her usual spot on the couch, logging onto her Call of Duty game, and I went up the stairs to my room.

Undressing, I climbed into the tub and reached for my knife. Leaning my head back, I closed my eyes and let memories of the Battle of Uruk flood my mind. The sounds of clashing weapons and cries of pain echoed in my thoughts as I drew the blade deeply across my throat, severing my vocal cords. Hot

33

blood spilled over my hand and down my breasts as I laid my knife on the edge of the tub. My lungs filled with the hot, coppery liquid, and my mind drifted to images of impaled and disemboweled Sumerians, their screams merging with the rush of darkness that claimed me.

***

The morning came with the familiar itch of dried blood. Pushing to my feet, I tossed my knife into the sink from the tub before closing the curtain. I turned on the water and began my routine of washing away last night's therapy from my skin. Once I was clean, I turned off the water and got out, drying one foot at a time before fully stepping out of the tub. Dropping the towel, I walked to the pedestal sink, washed my blade, sharpened it, and returned it to its place in the shower.

After getting dressed, I walked downstairs to find Theia passed out on the couch surrounded by empty bottles of tequila on the makeshift coffee table from an old steamer trunk. It was much quicker to just slit your throat, in my opinion. I picked up the two empty bottles and walked into the kitchen to get a cup of coffee, thankful she'd remembered to set it up before getting too drunk. After pouring myself a cup, I poured another for Theia and added a healthy splash of Irish liquor. Walking into the living room with both, I set hers on the table before shaking her shoulder.

Groaning, she opened one eye and glared at me. "Do I smell coffee?"

"Irish," I answered before taking a drink of my black coffee.

"I love you, you beautiful bitch." She pushed up into a sitting position and reached for the coffee.

34

"You act like your hangover won't be gone by the time you finish that cup," I said as I sat beside her on the worn couch.

"You act like a fifteen-minute headache isn't that bad, but it is." She took a drink of her coffee and hummed in appreciation. "How's your leg? You going to be able to move quickly without shit ripping up under the skin?"

"It's tight, not sore," I answered.

"I don't understand how you can heal so much faster than us." She said bitterly, her eyes still closed.

"I was born first," I said simply. Honesty, I hypothesized that my accelerated healing had something to do with my constant healing before becoming immortal. While my sisters were strong, I was athletically built from my decade of fighting for the king.

"Do you think we should split up today to look for her? Cover more ground?"

"Take a gun and a machete." I wasn't entirely comfortable with the idea of my sister being alone, but I knew the chances that we would just end up fighting again were high. After we finished off the whole pot of coffee and grabbed sandwiches to eat on the go, we left.

***

I'd been in the swamp for hours with no sign of Kassie when the sound of wolves in the distance reached my ears as I continued my fruitless search. Straightening, I listened, feeling my heart quicken. The howls weren't from normal wolves but from Lycans. "Damn it!" I cursed as I turned toward the howls, toward Theia. Bigfoot had better keep Kassie safe because there was no way Theia could take on a pack of Lycans alone. Even the two of us against them weren't good odds. Being the daughters of

35

that cock-sucker, Ares, was the only advantage we had, giving us more strength than regular Sirens.

Pushing through the swamp as fast as possible, I cursed the muck that slowed my speed. The sound of my labored breathing filled my ears, the howling of the wolves quickly drowning out the squishing sounds of my feet as I pushed through the swamp. How close were they to Theia? Could she hold them off until I got there? As long as I could hear the howling, there was hope that she was still alive and fighting.

As my foot snagged on a hidden root, I pitched forward into the muddy swamp floor. The sudden silence was deafening. "No!" I screamed, shoving myself back to my feet, mud, and moss clogging my mouth. Horror clenched in my gut. *Please let Theia have killed them!* I surged forward, mud and debris clinging to me, but I didn't care. I had to reach my sister. I couldn't be alone. For the second time since leaving Atlantis, fear gripped me, twisting my stomach into knots as I stumbled through the swamp.

Chapter 4

Ella...

"**D**amn it, make some fucking noise!" I huffed out and continued in the direction I'd heard the howling before the silence. The usual ruckus of the swamp seemed louder than ever as I struggled to hear any trace of my sister. "Theia!" I yelled, hoping she would hear me and respond.

Time seemed to crawl as I pushed forward, panic clawing at my chest. I continued to call out for Theia with no response. For once, my voice was filled with desperation, a tone I hadn't heard from myself in millennia. After what seemed like hours, I came upon a gory scene. Grunch and Lycans lay on the swamp floor, blood painting the green and brown moss a deep crimson. One Grunch remained, the head of a Lycan in its hands.

The horrible creature turned its gaze on me, and I charged forward with a snarl. My blade sliced through its neck with ease, ending the fight before it had begun. Panting, I scanned the area frantically, my heart pounding in my chest.

Theia was nowhere to be seen, causing me to look over my shoulder and into the surrounding trees. It was unlike Lycans to attack in silence, as their howls were used to drown out a

37

Siren's call, but that didn't mean it wasn't possible. Closing my eyes, I forced myself to take a deep breath and listen. The usual sounds of the swamp were all that met my ears. If wolves were close, the wildlife would alert me. Opening my eyes, I decided to focus on the mess before me.

I moved from one body to the next, assessing if any were a threat, only to find each creature decapitated. The hideous claws on the Grunch had separated the heads from the three Lycans before I'd ever made it here. Three more Grunch lay dead among the Lycans, totaling four of the vicious creatures.

Standing, I turned and examined the area more carefully. Blood was everywhere, the moss and mud torn up as evidence of a brutal fight. A chunk of flesh caught my eye, and I moved to it, picking it up. Turning the bloody piece over in my hand, I realized it was vocal cords. A Lycan attack strategy—rip out the vocal cords of a Siren, and they can't enchant you. I dropped my sister's flesh with a sickening splat and scanned the area for more clues, my ears still tuned to the surrounding sounds. I could see her boot prints, marks that looked as though she'd fallen to her hands and knees, followed by no more humanoid tracks.

One of the Lycans must have taken her, but why hadn't it stayed to help its pack? Two possibilities came to mind. The first: Theia had managed to enchant it before it tore out her vocal cords. The second: other Lycans were on their way to retrieve their fallen comrades, and the one that took Theia had its own reasons—reasons only the Gods knew. Deciding that taking on a pack of Lycans alone was a bad idea, I turned and headed back toward the fanboat we'd used to get out here. If Theia had enchanted the Lycan, she would return home as soon as she came

38

to and could command it. I had to remain logical, especially with both of my sisters now missing.

I navigated the waterways back to the manor in silence. Back in Atlantis, I'd been alone and weak. While I was alone now, I was no longer weak. My decade of fighting had hardened me long before I'd gained immortality. It was only a matter of time before I tracked down my sisters, and we were reunited. But deep down, that fragile part of me—the part locked away in the dark, filthy cell where I had spent countless hours recovering in Atlantis—was terrified. What if my sisters were no more? What if I failed them?

The hardened part of me refused to accept that. Still, I couldn't stop the thought from creeping in: if the worst came to pass, I would find a way to end my miserable existence. I'd only been living for my sisters since that first night at the mercy of the King. Without them, there would be nothing left for me.

Pulling the boat up to the dock, I forced myself to abandon the hopeless thoughts. Those would be left on the water, no longer allowed to linger in my mind. It was how I had survived all this time—by pushing my darkest fears to the back of my mind and focusing solely on the task at hand. It was my greatest strength and my only way forward.

After tying up the boat, I walked into the empty manor and grabbed my phone. A few calls later, I had a list of immortal bounty hunters for hire from the only agency I trusted not to send an assassin after my sisters and me. Gritting my teeth, I selected the safest option: Finlay Brown, a male Vampire.

"Just a moment while I connect the call," the digitized voice on the other end said. I had to hand it to the agency—they

39

made sure no one could trace their real identities, using a voice system that converted typed words into speech. Should a human somehow stumble across their number, they had safeguards in place, sending a person in a costume—usually a Witch or some other immortal who could pass for human.

"This is Fin, how may I be of assistance?" The masculine voice was smooth and professional.

"My sister is missing, and I have reason to believe she was abducted by Lycans," I said, keeping my tone steady. "I need someone capable of tracking her down and handling an altercation with unknown numbers if it comes to that. I can provide weapons to help eliminate the threat. One more thing—do you have a female I should be concerned about in your life?"

"I'm an unbonded male; there's no female to cause issues with the assignment. May I ask what kind of immortal you are so I can assess your strength level, should we end up in said altercation?" he asked.

"I am the daughter of a War God and a Siren," I replied flatly, seeing no need to offer my name.

"Then I have little concern about future altercations. When do I start?"

I gave him my address and asked how soon he could arrive, satisfied to hear he'd make it before sunrise. The sooner I could begin the search for Theia, the better. After hanging up, I immediately set to work preparing for the mission. Grabbing a bag, I packed a few changes of clothes and Theia's toiletries—just in case. Then, I pulled out a larger bag for weapons.

While my sisters hated relying on firearms during hunts, we still owned an impressive arsenal. I filled the weapons bag

40

with an assortment of handguns, two shotguns, four machetes, throwing stars, an array of knives, a few small explosives, and several bear traps. I included a case containing a disassembled sniper rifle and stand, knowing it could come in handy. My philosophy had always been that one could never be too prepared. For good measure, I tossed in a stun gun—it was always a solid option for interrogations. Finally, I topped off the bag with a crossbow and a full quiver of bolts.

Once my weapons were ready, I headed to the walk-in pantry in the kitchen. Digging through my stash of herbal extracts, I found the ones I needed: wolfsbane and vervain. Though not lethal to Lycans or Vampires, these herbs caused significant pain and, in high concentrations, could even induce hallucinations. They were perfect for coating the tips of my arrows or the edges of my blades.

Turning off the pantry light with its pull string, I returned to the living room and opened the leather-and-canvas-wrapped steamer trunk we used as a coffee table. Reaching inside, I pulled out the case of empty darts and syringes. I filled the white-feathered darts with wolfsbane extract and carefully placed them into their holder, designed to drape easily across my chest. Next, I filled a couple of medium-sized syringes, one filled specifically with vervain as a contingency plan in case the Vampire I'd hired needed to be neutralized.

After closing the lid of the old trunk, the metal clasps clattered noisily. I loaded a dart into the gun and set it alongside the rest of the wolfsbane-filled supplies. With that done, I returned to the kitchen to stow the remaining vervain extract in a cabinet. Back in the living room, I settled on the couch and

41

methodically inspected my weapons. Everything was accounted for. My supply of wolfsbane would need restocking once I got my sisters back, but for now, the priority was tracking down Theia's abductors and eradicating them.

Leaning back on the cream-colored couch with its faded stripes and floral pattern, I glanced outside. The efficiency of my preparation had left me with a couple of hours until sunset. Standing, I entered the kitchen and pulled a pizza from the freezer. If I was going to keep my strength up, I had to eat. After tossing the pizza in the oven, I grabbed a notebook and pen from the counter and sat at the kitchen table to write.

The first letter was to Kassie, detailing everything I knew about Theia's disappearance and my plan to find her. Before the Vampire and I left, she needed to be informed in case she returned tonight or tomorrow. Flipping to a new page, I wrote out the terms of my arrangement with the Vampire. The clarity of laying it all out gave me some comfort—I wasn't one to leave things to chance.

When I finished the letters, I sat back and let my gaze fall on the vervain-filled syringe. Finlay was an unbonded male Vampire, which meant he had no interest in the flesh, beyond the blood coursing beneath it. Still, unease flickered in my chest.

"Damn it, Ella, get it together," I muttered under my breath, forcing myself to confront the source of my discomfort. Finlay wasn't a threat to me—not in the way I feared most. Pain and death didn't scare me. A man's lustful advances, though, stirred a storm of emotions—fear, anger, and memories I'd buried long ago.

42

I stared at the syringe for a few long moments before sighing heavily. Vampires and zombies were the only males I trusted even slightly, and I had to trust this one if I was going to find Theia and keep myself composed.

But my usual way of coping—severing my vocal cords—wasn't an option. If I cut them now, I could still be in the middle of healing when he arrived. Worse, I would leave myself vulnerable if Lycans stumbled across my unconscious body. I needed someone here to guard me, and what better way to pay a Vampire than with blood I wasn't even using?

43

Chapter 5

Fin…

The home I arrived at was a small, whitewashed manor. Killing the engine, I stepped out of my black Sierra and walked toward the slightly run-down structure. As I neared the steps, a strange pain spread through my chest, causing me to frown in confusion. The moment my boot touched the first step of the porch, the screen door opened, and a female emerged.

Suddenly, my lungs felt like they were on fire, and my heart felt as though it were exploding. For the first time in five hundred years, I drew air into my lungs, and my heart began to beat. The female who had stepped onto the porch was my destined mate.

Shit.

She was compact and agile, standing around five feet six inches tall. Despite her smaller stature, there was an undeniable strength and confidence about her. Her frame was lean and well-muscled, evidence of a life spent in physical training. Sharp, defined features gave her a fierce look, accentuated by striking gray-blue eyes that seemed to pierce through the darkness. Her

44

hair, a cascade of dark waves, fell just past her shoulders, framing a face etched with determination.

"Are you Finlay?" Her steady and calm voice rang out as light glinted off the blade in her hand. Her no-nonsense attitude was mirrored by her practical attire: dark, durable fabrics, tactical pants, and a fitted top that allowed freedom of movement.

"Yes, but I prefer Fin. Are you Aella?" I asked, frozen in place as my mind reeled at the revelation that I'd found my mate.

"Eye-ell-uh, not A-ell-uh. I prefer Ella. I'm the Siren who hired you, Vampire," she replied, her voice carrying the cold melody of a blade sliding across a sharpening stone. A Siren. Right. I'd never encountered one before, but they were infamous for their ability to enchant men. Perhaps my heart and lungs were reacting to her immortal magic. "Come in," she said flatly before turning and walking back inside.

Taking a deep breath—one that burned like hell—I climbed the rest of the steps and followed her into what appeared to be the living room. "We discussed my assisting you in tracking your sister over the phone. Am I to assume we'll be leaving immediately?" I asked, struggling to ignore the burning ache as my once-shriveled lungs expanded and contracted, adjusting to their renewed purpose.

"No. We'll leave tomorrow evening, as soon as the sun is low enough for you to travel," she replied, her tone bland, almost bored. "Follow me, and I'll show you where you can rest. The curtains should be heavy enough to block the sunlight sufficiently."

"I appreciate the consideration of my condition," I said, trying to sound composed while still wrestling with the sensations

45

of my heart beating and blood flowing painfully through my body. I followed her down a hallway and into a bedroom just off the staircase. The rest of my organs seemed to awaken slowly, painfully reacting to the sudden return of blood flow; the experience was excruciating.

"I have no use for your ashes. You may use Kassie's bed to sleep; she hasn't returned yet." She turned and walked toward another door.

"Is this Kassie the reason we're waiting?" I questioned as she opened the door, revealing a bathroom.

"In part," she responded. "While you're under my employ, you'll have one other job to perform," she said, standing in the bathroom doorway. With a swift motion, she pulled her shirt over her head. "I'll pay you separately for this task." She reached behind her and unclasped her bra. I felt like I was going to combust as I forced my eyes to stay on her face. Here she was—possibly my destined female—stripping in front of me as if it were nothing. "Make sure no one comes through this door," she said, dropping her bra before stepping into the bathroom and closing the door.

I blew out a gust of breath that I'd been holding as she'd started to undress. Either she was extremely confident in her sexuality, or she knew unbonded Vampires couldn't get aroused. Unfortunately, I was the exception. I was hard as a rock. Standing outside the bathroom door, I struggled to calm myself, but my mind raced. Was my heart beating because she truly was mine? Or was this simply the power of a Siren—a force few immortals could resist? The questions gnawed at me as I remained on guard, my instincts sharp despite my inner turmoil.

46

Minutes passed before the sharp, metallic scent of blood filled my nostrils, cutting through my thoughts like a blade. Alarm shot through me as I reached for the bathroom door handle without hesitation. I burst into the room to find her lying in the tub, her throat slit deep and blood pooling around her. Her arm hung limply over the edge, blood trickling from a sliced wrist into a bowl on the floor. My eyes darted to a neatly written note placed beside the bowl.

Vampire,

If you are half the mercenary you're supposed to be, then you've smelled my blood and come in, without knocking, prick. The bowl is clean and intended to catch your payment for this task. Once the bleeding stops, feel free to help yourself. I'm not using that blood anymore, anyway.

-Aella

I dropped the note and stared at her in open-mouthed horror. She'd slit her own throat and left me to guard her as she bled out. "Bloody hell," I breathed as I leaned against the wall. What was I supposed to do? At least this answered my earlier question, I thought. If she weren't mine, then her 'death' would, in theory, have stopped the beating of my heart. But my heart was still pounding in my ears.

I glanced at her, then at the note in my hands. I would wait for her to regain consciousness, then demand an explanation. Until then, I scanned the room for a towel. Once the bleeding stopped, I'd turn on the shower and rinse away her blood. Her nudity made me oddly uncomfortable. I wanted to look at my female, but looking at her without her knowing she was mine felt wrong. That was until I noticed the scars.

47

Crouching next to the tub, I took in her body with a clinical detachment rather than a lustful gaze. Scars were scattered all over her arms, legs, and torso. There was very little of her that wasn't marked by evidence of violence. Being immortal meant these wounds had occurred before she'd reached her immortality. Anger bubbled inside me at the thought that she—or any female—had endured such treatment. I wondered how many times this small female had been near death, and my anger surged even more.

Gaining my feet, I leaned forward and turned on the shower. Seeing as she'd severed both the artery in her neck and in her wrist, her heart had stopped beating before I'd even found the towel. Running a hand through my hair, I watched as the blood rinsed off her body, wondering how I was going to clean her up. I badly wanted to touch her, to run my fingers over her scars, to will her wounds away, but touching a female without her permission was something I'd never done.

Looking at the showerhead, I was relieved to find it was detachable. Quickly grabbing the sprayer, I set to work rinsing the blood away before turning off the water. After drying my hands on the towel, I draped it over her body, covering as much of her as I could. Seeing that her nudity was covered and her blood washed away, I sat on the floor with my back to the wall and waited for her to regain consciousness.

Ella...

When I came to, I was still lying in the tub, but my hair was damp, a towel was covering me, and the Vampire glared at me from the floor. I sat up and looked down at the towel. "Did my

48

nudity offend you?" Probably because of his impotence, it was the only thing that made up for him being male.

"Once you stopped bleeding, I turned the shower on and rinsed you off. I thought you might like to have a towel to dry yourself once you came to," he said tightly. His jaw clenched as he glared at me. "Why the hell did you slit your throat?" he demanded.

"I have my reasons," I replied in my distorted, near-whisper of a voice, my vocal cords not yet fully healed. I leaned back in the tub. There was no reason for me to take a defensive stance—he wasn't a threat, not with his lack of a pulse. Reminding myself of that had been the only thing that enabled me to strip in front of him earlier.

"I asked a direct question and was hoping for a more direct answer," he said through gritted teeth.

I narrowed my eyes. "I'm not paying you to interrogate me. I'm paying you to help me find my sisters and, separately, to protect me while I'm unconscious."

"You were fucking dead! You slit your bloody throat—not just a neat little cut, but deep! Why the hell would anyone mutilate themselves like that?" His voice rose as frustration bled into his words.

"I had an itch to scratch. If you have a problem with that, then I will find another Vampire to help me," I said with disinterest.

"Fuck," he muttered, shoving himself to his feet. "I've been hired by a lunatic." He stalked toward the door, but before leaving, he turned back. "And for the record, I don't drink blood from a fucking bowl like a dog."

49

Rolling my eyes, I pulled the towel up and began drying my hair. "You are as moody as my sisters."

He cleared his throat and deliberately turned his back to me. "Could you warn me before getting naked?"

"Are you that upset with your impotence that seeing a naked female upsets your delicate sensibilities?" For once, I was amused by a male.

"Not exactly," he replied, still not facing me. "Have you ever been around a male Vampire before? An unbonded one, I mean?"

"Yes," I said cautiously, narrowing my eyes at his back. "Why?"

"Right. So it's *normal* for you to just strip in front of Vampires because they can't get it up. Got it."

"You could leave the bathroom if it upsets you that much," I said, relaxing. He was just insecure about his dysfunctional manhood.

"I need to talk to you when you're fully clothed," he replied before walking out and closing the door behind him.

If the Vampire was going to help me find my sister, I needed to make things very clear to him. After getting dressed, I walked out of the bathroom and found him pacing the bedroom. "Look, Vampire, the only redeeming quality of your manhood is that your *manhood* is impotent. Males are lustful creatures who should be eradicated from existence, in my opinion. A male's lust makes him untrustworthy and disrespectful. Lust drives a male to take what he wants without permission and without regard for others. While humans have evolved to speak, the males of our species have not evolved past their animalistic urges."

50

He looked at me for a moment before carefully replying, "If you believe Vampires feel no lust simply because they have no heartbeat, you've been lied to. Being unable to have an erection does not negate one's ability to feel attraction or admiration for a well-built specimen. If we're speaking in clinical terms."

Narrowing my eyes at him, I tilted my head to the side, contemplating his words. "Then are you saying I am a *well-built specimen*?"

His gaze was clinical as he regarded me, taking in my face and then glancing over my stature. "You are comparable to a Greek statue—sturdy, beautiful, and chiseled."

"Fuck Greece," I muttered before turning to head out to the kitchen.

"I didn't compare you to a country, but sure, fuck Greece," he muttered, following me out of the room. He moved toward the shadows of the living room to avoid the sunlight spilling into the space.

If I could watch that country burn for all eternity, it wouldn't be enough to make up for the hell its people had put my sisters and me through. The Vampire's clinical description of me was refreshing, though. Unlike so many others, he hadn't compared me to a delicate island flower, as people often did with my sisters. I hated flowers.

"I hope your hatred of males doesn't put a damper on our relationship," the Vampire said from just outside the kitchen doorway, where the sunlight kept him at bay.

"Very observant of you. Do you drink coffee or just blood?" I asked, deliberately ignoring his question, mostly

51

because I didn't know the answer myself. Since reuniting with my sisters, I hadn't had to suffer the presence of a male alone.

He sighed. "I drink coffee but I can wait until the sun's low enough to get my own. You hired me, not the other way around."

"Or I could just close the curtains," I replied flatly. So much for him being observant. I moved to draw the curtains shut, blocking out the sunlight. He stepped into the kitchen, looking sheepish. His mild humiliation was oddly satisfying. A decade of enduring others taking pleasure in my humiliation at the hands of males had left me like this.

He opened the fridge as I hit the start button on the coffee pot. I turned to look at him in curiosity. Vampires didn't eat unless they'd found their destined female, and this one had told me he hadn't. He pulled out a carton of eggs. "How do you take your eggs?" he asked.

"Over easy, with bacon," I replied, narrowing my eyes. "Why are you cooking?"

"Just because I live on a liquid diet doesn't mean my clients do," he said, unfazed. "I can also enjoy smoothies, you know, because they're liquid. Speaking of, do you have a blender?"

"I will cook my own food. The blender is in the cabinet next to the fridge."

The Vampire sighed heavily, still not turning to look at me. The question that followed froze me in place. "Are you sure your powers can't affect Vampires?"

"Sirens can only affect those with a heartbeat," I said carefully, feeling threatened.

52

He bent over, pulled the blender from the cabinet, and set it on the counter, still avoiding my gaze. "I became a Vampire because of a female. She lured me into her bed, which wasn't hard; I was a young male, more than happy to find pleasure with a willing and beautiful partner. But the female I took to my bed wasn't some willing maid. She was one of the king's mistresses. When the king discovered our affair, he had me beaten and locked up. I thought for sure he'd have my head removed from my body, but instead, I was sentenced to hang. It was her doing—she told me this when she came to my cell. She tricked me into drinking her blood the night before I was to hang."

"Why are you telling me this?" I asked, my hackles still raised. I'd never asked how he became a Vampire, only if he was bonded.

"Because when I awoke in my grave to Colette digging me up, I hated her. I hated all females for the hold they have over males with just a coy smile or an arch of their backs. Colette cursed me to a death that wasn't death. She cursed me with a thirst for blood and a life in the shadows—all for the chance that I might be hers. When my heart did not beat, I was happy. My mind was clear, and I was freed from the cravings of the flesh. For five hundred years, I've lived with a new perspective on the world. Until I stepped foot on that bottom step yesterday and found myself looking at you."

I stood there, staring at him as he started the blender. What had he just told me? The angry grinding of the blender matched the chaos swirling in my mind. Could my powers affect Vampires? The blender stopped, and he began opening cabinets,

53

searching for a glass. "Top shelf, on the right," I told him in a daze.

He turned to face me, his expression firm. "I am an honest male. I have never forced a female into my bed or looked without permission. That's why you woke to find yourself covered with that towel. I ask that you don't conduct yourself so carelessly in front of me again. I am feeling things for you against my will, and you know as well as I do that being immortal is a curse. You made it perfectly clear when you came out of the bathroom that you have no use for men. I will keep our relationship professional, but I cannot abide you cutting your throat."

I blinked at him, stunned by his words before anger surged to the surface. "I will do whatever the hell I want, Vampire." I sneered the word like an insult, contemplating throwing open the curtains to drive him from the room.

"Then I wish you the best of luck finding your sister," he replied coldly, his tone cutting like a blade. Picking up his smoothie—filled with Gods only knew what—he turned and walked out of the room.

Shock froze me in place for a moment. Never had a male walked away from me so coldly, so detached. A flush of indignation overtook me as I strode after him. "I hired you for a job, and it's not done yet," I snapped.

He stopped, turning back with an expression that brimmed with restrained anger. "Even I have my limits. You refuse to give me a reason for your self-mutilation, and I simply cannot stand by and watch it happen to you again."

"What right do you have to tell me what I can and cannot do?" I demanded, my voice sharp and biting.

54

"None—that's why I will leave if you continue to carve out your throat like some deranged animal!" he shot back.

I blinked, surprised by his answer, and just stared at him. "I can't stop," I said simply.

A look of pure rage darkened his features, but his voice was calm and deadly when he spoke. "Who has cursed you with this? A Witch? What magical being has taken your choice from you?"

"What? No, that's not what I meant." For the first time, I was faltering, my stone facade crumbling under the relentless questioning of one measly Vampire.

"Then tell me why you cannot stop. Why must you cause yourself harm if not for the interference of some malicious person?" he demanded, his tone sharp and unyielding.

"It stops the itch," I said quietly, my voice devoid of its usual confidence. Why was I telling him this?

"What bloody itch? What kind of itch demands a blade across your throat?" he raged, the calculated calm of his voice vanishing, replaced by raw desperation and anger.

"My vocal cords," I snapped, my defenses rising instinctively. "If you could deny your hunger by ripping out your fangs, would you?"

His expression wavered, torn between confusion and fury. "What?"

I clenched my fists at my sides, my body tensing as if preparing for an attack. "Would you rip out your own fangs to stop the thirst, Vampire?" I pressed, my voice turning sharp and bitter.

55

"I'm not going to fight you," he said, taking a step back, his posture deliberately nonthreatening.

"I'm not some delicate lady," I sneered. "A decade at the hands of gladiators, fighting males twice my size has made me stronger than you, Vampire."

"What?" he asked, baffled, still backing away until he accidentally stepped into a ray of sunlight. A hiss of pain escaped him as he recoiled from the light.

"You never answered my question, Vampire," I said, my tone cutting. "If you could control your thirst for blood by ripping out your own fangs, would you?"

His eyes widened as realization dawned. "You sever your vocal cords because you can't control your Siren power. You're enslaved to it."

"Not so stupid after all, for a male," I said coldly as I returned to the kitchen where I'd left my cup of coffee. To my surprise, he didn't follow me. I opened the cabinet I'd stashed the vervain in and sat at the table with the bottle in front of me. Pulling my knife from my pocket as he walked in, I opened the bottle and dipped my blade as I looked up at him. "Should I assume that you know what vervain does to Vampires?"

"It weakens us," he said, not moving as he watched me close the bottle once more.

"Yes. This is a concentrated extract, which means it's far more effective. Over the years, I've learned that some Vampires are stronger than others, or have tried to build a tolerance to vervain. Should you cross me, I will not hesitate to sink this blade into your heart and remove your head from your body," I said,

56

rising from the table and stepping toward him, the knife's tip pointed at his chest.

"You have so little trust for me," he said, his voice calm but his eyes intense. "And yet, you leave yourself vulnerable for hours, unconscious after slitting your throat."

"Don't test me, Vampire," I warned, closing the distance and holding the blade just a hair's breadth from his throat.

He sighed and gently pushed my hand down. "As a hired bounty hunter and assassin, I'm used to clients not trusting me—and, frankly, I'm used to not trusting them. But this situation is… new," he said, sipping his smoothie and grimacing. "Apparently, having a heartbeat has also changed my taste in things."

I hated him. I hated that he was right. It made no sense for me to distrust him while leaving myself exposed. What was I going to do? If I didn't sever my vocal cords, I would lose control of my powers and inevitably entrap a male—him being the closest. But I had no time to find a willing female to satisfy the desires I despised. Anger toward my sisters flared, but I forced it back down. I lived only for them. For twelve millennia, I'd endured torment as a Siren, unable to deny the cravings of the flesh.

"How about I cover my ears when you need to let it out?" he said suddenly, pulling me from my thoughts. "That way, you don't entrap me, take care of the itch, and are not left vulnerable. I'd offer to let you stab me with that vervain or knock me out, but then I wouldn't be able to protect you."

"You truly know nothing of Sirens, do you, Vampire?"

57

"I insist you call me Fin," he replied. "I hate being a Vampire—it wasn't my choice. And no, I don't know much about your kind."

"Our singing isn't voluntary. It's forced upon us until our desires are met. The only way to delay the process is to injure the vocal cords. I've tried strangulation so I wouldn't lose consciousness, but they heal too quickly. The last time I lost control…" I paused, swallowing hard. "The beaches ran red with blood. While I enjoy a good battle, such carnage pleases Ares far too much."

"Ares?" Fin asked, his tone skeptical.

"Yes. Our bastard father—the god of war," I stated, walking back to the table and my coffee.

"Wait, you're the daughter of *Ares*?"

"The bastard child of a bastard immortal. My vocal cords must be severed," I replied, taking a sip.

Fin closed his eyes and tilted his head back toward the ceiling. "Very well. I'll think about how to tolerate this while we search for your sister."

"I'll find another Vampire to help me while you do that," I shot back, my tolerance for his presence already waning. If I didn't need help finding Theia, I'd have killed him by now.

"I'll kill any male who touches you without your permission," he said suddenly. "I don't trust other Vampires."

"You are a Vampire," I pointed out.

"Not by choice," he said, his voice firm. "And I was a man of honor before my death. Most are not—as you seem to have discovered." His eyes dropped briefly to the worst of my

58

scars, the ones carved across my stomach—the ones left from the removal of my reproductive organs.

"I trust no one but my sisters," I said, my voice final.

59

Chapter 6

Ella...

After our interaction in the kitchen, Fin dumped his smoothie, made something else to eat for himself, and went to the living room to sit in a dark corner on the floor. As I waited for the sun to get low enough for us to leave, I contemplated killing him at least a hundred different ways. Oddly enough, the Vampire seemed utterly uninterested in me. He sat on the floor, examined his food before taking a bite, and closed his eyes as he seemed to enjoy the food way too much. I glared at him for a few minutes before going into the kitchen, where I sat with the knife and ate my food, enjoying my bloodied imaginings of his death the way he seemed to enjoy his food.

I had long since finished my coffee and food when he entered the kitchen with his empty plate. "I'm guessing we have about half an hour or so before the sun is low enough for me to withstand it," he said as he began to wash his plate, still not looking at me.

Narrowing my eyes at his back, I wondered if his indifference to me was some sort of ploy. "Wash mine while

60

you're at it," I told him, shoving my plate and cup forward on the table.

"I suppose that's fair, considering I wasted that smoothie." I shoved myself up from the table so fast I nearly toppled the chair and walked out of the kitchen. "What? What'd I say?" he asked from behind me.

"Fucking male! Just my fucking luck," I gritted out as I stormed out the door and onto the front porch. "My bloody father probably has something to do with this! I just know it! The fates couldn't just give me a damned break for once in my miserable existence!"

"You know I can hear every word you're saying, right?" Fin's voice came from the shadows inside.

"Fuck off, Leech," I snapped, itching to fight.

"Suit yourself," he muttered and disappeared deeper into the shadows of the house.

I roared and punched the white column that was the support beam of the porch, watching it crack. His indifference was infuriating! How could he be so damned calm? Looking off into the distance, I wondered where Kassie was. If I had Kassie, this wouldn't be so unbearable. The feeling of hopelessness washed over me, followed by anger. This wasn't supposed to happen! I was an immortal warrior! I'd hardened myself to stone, cold and unfeeling, yet here I was, wanting to rage and cry at the same time. How had I lost both my sisters in less than a week when we'd not been separated for even a single night in over twelve thousand years?

Walking to the railing, I stared off into the distant trees. I didn't even know how to live without my sisters. Could I trust the

61

Vampire to keep me safe while I was unconscious? No, but I didn't have a choice. If I didn't cut my vocal cords, then I would inevitably end up entrapping Fin, seeing as he was the closest male. My body craved some sort of release, but I refused to obtain that release from a male.

"I know you hate me and all, but we should probably discuss our plans before it's time to actually move," the Vampire's voice came from the shadows inside my home once again.

"Once the sun is low enough, I'll take you to where my sister was captured, and we will head out in that direction."

"That's probably just going to be a waste of time. Trust me, I know how Lycans work. They have safehouses all over the world and bars that they frequent. Most of the time, you can pick up their trail at one of the bars. If your sister is alive, she's being held under lock and key in one of those houses."

My jaw clenched as I mulled over what he'd said. "What if you're wrong? What if she's out there somewhere in the bayou?"

"Then she would have shown up here already, judging by the rate you healed. We can go and follow the tracks if you'd like; you are the one who hired me."

After thinking for a moment, I decided he might be right. "I'm leaving a note for my other sister. When she contacts us to find out where we are, I will send her to check the tracks. One way or another, I will find Theia."

"Going at the hunt from two angles is always a good idea. Are you sure your sister will be safe following those tracks alone?"

62

"I have a feeling she won't be alone," I muttered as I glared at the trees.

"Is there something you're not telling me?"

"Nothing you need to worry about, Leech," I told him. Once Kassie reached out to me, I would figure out what to do from there. The less time I was stuck with the Vampire, the better.

I heard him sigh heavily from inside. "I get that you don't like males at all, but I'm not in the habit of getting myself killed by clients."

"Clearly."

"The closest bar I know of that Lycans frequent is about an hour away. I will go and make some calls and find out if anyone has seen any Lycans traveling with a female, but I'll need to know what your sister looks like."

"There is a picture on her profile. She's an online gamer."

"You could be a little more helpful and a little less hateful. Even though you caused my damn heart to start again, I'm not interested in anything other than a job."

"Good to know. The remote is on the TV; I'm sure you can figure it out," I shot back. There was no way I was going inside with him. If I had to describe my sister, I'd say she was a sexy gamer. Theia had tattoos and piercings, and her hair changed color as often as we moved. It wouldn't surprise me if she shaved half her head off like the mortals have started doing the next time we moved. Kassie would be the one to help her do it, though—Kassie is good with hair.

I don't know how long I stood on the porch thinking about my sisters, but Fin pulled me out of my thoughts. "The sun is low

63

enough that I should be all right as long as I keep most of my skin covered. Shall we go into the swamp and take a look?"

"Didn't you say that would be a waste of time?"

He sighed. "I didn't get any leads while I was on the phone. That means the best option is to figure out what direction they went. I may not have been looking in the right area to start."

"Do you think he would take her to a bar?"

Fin shrugged. "I'm not sure. He may be the kind to brag and show off what he sees as his newest possession. He could also be getting her as far from here as possible before making any stops. I don't know why a Lycan or Werewolf would take your sister."

"They have been hunting us, trying to eradicate us from existence for centuries. Why the dog didn't just kill her, I don't know, nor do I care. I just want my sister back, and then I'll take my revenge on who I see fit."

"I do not doubt that," he said dryly.

"I don't trust you, Vampire."

"Then allow me to be completely transparent; I don't trust you either. Being close to you is torture because it stirs feelings in my body that are distracting and unwelcome. I have the urge to protect you and rip apart all those who have harmed you. That being said, it's really none of my damn business who hurt you. Had you not caused my heart to start beating again, I wouldn't feel these things. I would do my job and get paid. Now, thanks to you, I get to experience the rush of life all over again. And you know what? Life fucking sucks. The sooner we get this job done, the sooner I can get away from you and stop my damn heart again."

64

"I could always rip it out if it's that much of a problem."

"Maybe later. Right now, we have a dog to track," he said dismissively as he walked to the steps and gestured for me to lead the way. *Fucking Leech.*

My eyes narrowed as I marched by him and down the steps. Without looking back to see if he was following, I made my way to the boat and untied it. Fin stepped on and took a seat in silence. After getting everything ready, I started up the fan and began navigating the waterways to where Theia and I had been just yesterday. Just yesterday, my sister and I were together. Just a few days ago, all three of us were together and bickering the way we do. Now I was alone with a Vampire who claimed me as his female.

"I found the evidence of her fight in this part of the swamp. It was a mess when I was here yesterday," I told Fin as I brought the boat to a stop and found a tree to tie it to. We got off the boat, and I led him into the swamp until we reached the area where I'd found my sister's vocal cords. "From what I can tell, whoever took her went that way."

"From what I can tell, you're right. Not that I'd expect anything less after meeting you."

"Glad to see I've made an impression," my tone was dry as I responded to him.

"Not the kind most make, but yes, you've made an impression," he said without looking at me. The Vampire walked around the area, looking at every little detail and taking it all in. "It looks like I was calling in the right direction; these tracks are headed north. Short of following these tracks, there is no way to tell if their direction has changed. We have two options." Fin

65

turned to face me then. "We can follow these tracks and probably lose the trail because it is a swamp. Or we can get in my truck, head toward the bar I was telling you about, and start searching for clues in that area."

"You already called the bars, didn't you?"

"I did, but I didn't get to talk to the people inside that bar, nor did I get to talk to gas stations or other places they may have stopped."

I gritted my teeth. "Fine, let's go."

"Glad to see you're going to be a blast in the hour-long ride there," he said with sarcasm as he headed back to the boat.

"It's good to see you've picked up on American slang despite your British accent."

"England, America, it's all the same: a place to hide in the shadows and get paid."

When we returned to the manor, the sun had fully set. "Just let me get my bags, and we can head out."

"And here I was thinking you were different from other females," he muttered as he walked to his truck. When I came back out, I had a backpack with a few changes of clothes inside and my duffle bag full of weapons. I handed the duffle to him. He hefted the bag into the back seat of his truck and then turned to look at me. "It feels and sounds like weapons. I'd also wager that your backpack has a few more inside. I do hope you brought some clothing, though. I have no idea how long we will be looking for your sister."

"I'm not an idiot," I said with a glare before climbing into the passenger seat.

"Everything is going to be a fight with you, isn't it?"

66

"Just drive, Leech." He rolled his eyes before putting the truck in reverse and turning around to leave the driveway.

As we left the manor behind, I couldn't help but wonder if Kassie was indeed all right. What were the chances that both of my sisters were in equal amounts of danger and I was being forced to pick between them?

"Have you ever tried to hit your vocal cords without fully severing your throat?" Fin broke the silence only about twenty minutes into the trip.

I sighed heavily and glanced at him. "The smaller the wound, the faster I heal. I would assume you would know this, being an immortal."

"I've never seen anyone heal as quickly as you from that extensive of a wound either," he muttered.

"You'd think it would be a good thing to heal as quickly as we do."

"Not if your injury is the only thing keeping you from being forced to do something you hate. Although I'm not sure if hate is a strong enough word for someone willing to carve out their own throat."

"How touching—you sympathize." The sarcasm dripped from my words.

"I still don't like it, but who would like walking in to find their employer bleeding out in a bathtub and being told to drink from a bowl like a stray dog?"

"I find joy in your discomfort," I replied, my tone bland and uninterested.

"That's what joy sounds like? I have to wonder what boredom sounds like," he returned in a sarcastic tone.

67

Leaning forward, I turned on the radio.

"We're all done talking then, I guess."

"Yes."

He leaned forward and turned down the radio another twenty minutes or so down the road. "When we go in, it may be best if you keep quiet about you being a Siren."

"Don't worry about me, Leech, just do your job."

He sighed. "Sure, I see we're sticking with calling me a leech."

"How much further?" I asked, ignoring his comment. I owed him nothing.

"Look up there; you can see it already," he pointed ahead of us and to the left. There was a neon sign saying 'Private Club.' The closer we got, I noticed a strange appearance on the sign before I realized there was a magic mark on the sign. "It took me a while to figure out that Lycans favored these bars with that mark. Access to the entrance is restricted for mortals unless they are marked in some way."

"Marked?"

He glanced at me and then back at the road. "I've run into a few immortals who take mortals as, sort of, pets. Sadly, a lot of them are Vampires. The Vampire's claim they intend to turn them when the human is ready, but I don't believe them."

"Are you saying you've never turned anyone?" I asked as we pulled into the parking lot.

"Never," he said, parking the truck and turning it off. "Let's get this out of the way. If it turns out to be a dead end, I want to go to some gas stations and see what we can find. If the

68

attendants are human, I might be able to just get them to believe I'm a private investigator."

"If the attendants are male, I can hum, and they will do whatever the fuck I want."

"Right, on that note, let's start bar hopping."

I exited the truck and began walking to the bar without sparing him a glance. When I reached the door, a large male who smelled like teakwood looked down at me. "This is a private club," he said as he looked me over.

"I destroyed Atlantis, Gargoyle. Don't make me take your wings."

"She's with me," Fin said from behind me.

"Finlay, good to see you again. What has it been, fifty years?"

"I'm not sure, to be honest," Fin said as he glanced around.

"I'm guessing you're looking for someone?" the Gargoyle asked as he eyed me.

"Look at my tits again, motherfucker, and I'll relieve your head from your body."

"Good heavens," Fin said as he pinched the bridge of his nose.

The Gargoyle held up his hands in surrender. "No need to get rude. Looking everyone over for hidden weapons is my job, and you have a blade in your bra that's not allowed."

"I have one in each pocket and each boot as well," I said as I began to pull them all out and hand them over. "I expect each one back when I walk out."

"Larry, this is my newest client, Ella. You wouldn't happen to have seen a Lycan and a pretty chick with piercings and tattoos, green eyes, and highlighted hair?"

"So the chick is the target? No, I haven't, but I just got back from vacation today. Go on in and check with the customers; most of them are regulars. Oh, and what kind of immortal are you?" Larry asked, nodding at me.

"She's the daughter of Ares," Fin answered for me, and I glared at him.

"No shit? Explains the temper. Try not to start a war in the bar; I gotta clean that shit up."

Chapter 7

Ella...

"Why don't you just stay quiet while I ask questions?" Fin suggested as we walked in.

"Go fuck yourself. I'll take the left; you take the right. The faster we get answers, the faster we get rid of each other," I said as I walked to the right and tapped the first female on the shoulder I saw.

She turned around and looked me over before biting her bottom lip. "You want my number or something?"

"Yeah, something. I'm looking for a Lycan who took something from me. He's traveling with a female about my height with tattoos, piercings, and blue highlights. Comes off as a total bitch."

"Oh sugar, did a Lycan steal your girlfriend?" she asked with a giggle.

"No, but I'm glad you picked up on the fact that I like cats instead of dogs. Shame you smell like you just sucked a cock, though," I wrinkled my nose. "Salty and sour."

"You bitch!"

71

"That's what my sisters say. Enjoy your night," I said as I walked away.

"I'm not done with you," she snapped as she grabbed my shoulder.

I spun around and grabbed a fistful of her hair, bringing her face to mine. "How about a taste for the road then?" I muttered before locking lips with hers.

She shoved me back, her face burning bright red. "That's not how you seduce someone!"

I shrugged and replied, "Your loss. I am looking for that Lycan and his pet, though." Calling my sister a pet made my stomach turn, but I knew that if this were a Lycan bar, I had to pretend to not give a damn about my sister.

"None of the Lycans that have come in here the last few nights have had any pets with them. At least, not when they arrive," she added with a smirk.

"Ew," I said before walking away. I'd hoped that kissing her would ease the itch in my throat, but it had done nothing. It looked like I was going to have to figure something else out while I searched for my sister.

"Are we looking for your sister or a one-night stand?" Fin's voice came from behind me.

"You told me you didn't like my coping mechanism, so I tried to scratch the itch another way while getting answers."

"Really? What did you find out?"

"She hasn't seen any Lycans come in with anyone in the last few days, but they aren't going home alone either. Gag."

72

He sighed. "To be honest, I thought you were about to get in a fight, not shove your tongue down some random hooker's throat. I only got to ask one person before they pointed you out."

"Didn't mean to be a distraction," I said as I rolled my eyes and walked away to pick up a drink in front of another female. "Do you mind if I ask you about someone?" I asked as I swirled her drink and smelled it.

"I mind that you have my fucking drink," she said. Was it her that smelled fruity or the drink?

"Good, no bullshit with you then. You answer my questions, and I'll give this mixed shit back."

She huffed and crossed her arms. "Fine, what do you want to know?"

"Have you seen a female, tattoos, possible nose and lip rings? She may have gotten them ripped out, and highlights in her hair. Oh, and she'd be traveling with a Lycan."

"I haven't seen any Lycans tonight, and if I knew what kind of female you were looking for, it might be more helpful than that vague-ass description."

"What about last night?" I asked, trying to keep from punching the cunt in her face.

"I'm just passing through on the way to visit my sister's coven. This is literally the first time I've ever been here."

"Could you do a tracking spell?" Didn't Witches smell like cider?

"My sister's the Witch; I'm the Elf. My dad's a man-hoe. Are we done here?" she asked, holding her hand out for her drink back. Elf that explained the scent: Black currant and jasmine.

73

"I don't drink fruity shit anyway," I said as I sat her drink down and moved to the next female I saw. I repeated this process until I made my way back to Fin.

"Any luck?" he asked, looking frustrated.

"I got a couple of numbers I'll never call. Other than that, no."

"Let's go to the gas station down the road. We will hit as many as we can before we head for the safehouse," he said with a sigh.

I began walking for the door without him when someone slapped my ass. Anger flared as I spun around to take out the person who hit me, only to find Fin snapping the neck of the much larger male. He dropped to the floor before Fin, who cleared his throat and fixed his shirt. The bar fell silent around us. "What. The. Fuck." was all I could get out.

"No one assaults my clients. It's part of the agreement."

"So you take all the fucking fun out of it for me?" I yelled, dumbfounded.

He shrugged and stepped over the unconscious male. "He should wake up before sunrise if anyone is wondering. We'll see ourselves out now."

"You just broke my brother's neck," an equally large female said as she stood from a nearby table.

"I'd have ripped his fucking head off after having some fun kicking his overgrown ass," I said to what I suspected was some sort of Demon based on their smoky scents.

She smiled. "I've not seen anyone best my brother in one hundred years! Cheers to the puny Vampire!"

74

A single snort escaped me before I shook my head and turned to leave the bar, Fin hot on my heels.

"Laugh it up. You would have killed him, and we'd be dead right now," Fin defended.

"What the hell happened?" Larry asked as we walked outside.

"I broke the neck of a Demon," Fin muttered.

"My weapons," I cut in before Larry could ask more questions.

"You did what?" The Gargoyle ignored me.

"My blades, Gargoyle, now," I hissed, drawing his attention.

"He attempted to assault my client, and I neutralized him before she could kill him," Fin said, putting his hand into his pocket and pulling out a pack of gum.

Larry began handing me my blades as he asked, "What did he do to you that you were going to kill him?"

"Any male who touches me deserves to die."

"She hates males. Only employed me because Vampires don't have a pulse," Fin said.

"Yes, and you're just a puny Vampire," I reminded in my bland tone. Why I'd even said that was beyond me. My sisters were the only ones I ever joked with, yet I was prodding at him the same way I would with my sisters.

"Puny," Larry repeated with a chuckle.

"Looks can be deceiving," Fin said in a defensive tone glaring at me.

"Let's get moving. The sooner we find my sister, the sooner we can be done," I reminded him.

75

His jaw clenched. "My thoughts exactly." With that, he began walking to his truck, and I followed. His discomfort with me made him easier to tolerate. Perhaps that was why I'd joked with him? Or maybe I had no idea how to be alone with a male. Without my sisters, it was up to me to converse with him.

I was glad for the silence as we climbed into the truck. Fin didn't look at me as we pulled out and drove only a block away to the gas station. "Stay here. I'll run in and ask the questions," he said as he pulled up and put the truck in park. "It will be faster that way."

"Fine," was my response. It wasn't like I wanted to interact with anyone else tonight anyway. I'd already interacted with more beings than I liked. Closing my eyes, I leaned my head back as he got out of the truck. This may be one of the only times I would be able to relax in the coming days. I wasn't delusional; finding my sister would take more than a few hours. The real question was why the dog had taken her in the first place instead of just killing her. Did they know the three of us were together? Was she being held for information about us?

My eyes opened, and I stared at the ceiling of the truck. My time in Atlantis had hardened me against pain and torture. Over the years, Theia had shared some of her troubles from that decade with me. How would she hold up to being captive again? We didn't like to admit when we were weak, but each of us had our weaknesses. For me, I hated males because I'd been too weak to escape their torment. For Kassie, it was her heart that was her weakness. She'd grown attached repeatedly throughout our lives, and each time, she lost everyone but Theia and myself. Was there

76

anything the Lycans could honestly use against Theia without Kassie or me there?

The truck door opened, pulling me from my thoughts. "The attendant here tonight wasn't on duty last night, but she gave me the contact information for the two employees who were here yesterday and last night."

"No footage of the pumps?" I asked, hoping that we could get a lead from that.

"I couldn't get her to give that to me. The human pointed out that she didn't even have to talk to me when I asked about it without a warrant."

"If one of the others is a male, I suppose I can always entrap him and get the footage that way."

"Wouldn't that just cause him to want to please you?"

"I can control the volume of my power, as can my sisters, to only slightly influence males. It's easier to do with mortals. A small hum, and they will do whatever we say will make us happy," I told him. Glancing at him, I added, "With immortals, we normally just fully entrap them, and they die attempting to please us."

"That explains why Sirens aren't very popular among immortals," he said as he pulled out and drove to the next gas station.

"I'll go in this time," I said as he parked the truck.

"Fine, it's not like you hired me for this or anything."

"I hired you to assist me, not do the entire thing for me." I got out of the truck, walked into the gas station, and found a young male behind the counter playing on his phone. I was both pleased and displeased at his gender. There was another male

77

shopping down an aisle, much to my annoyance. Did I wait for the customer to leave or entrap them both? Walking to the refrigerators, I picked up a six-pack of beer and braced myself for what I was about to do.

As the refrigerator door slapped shut, I began to hum, calling on that tingling annoyance in my throat as I walked to the check-out counter. The sound of a bag of chips hitting the floor told me the customer had heard my dreadful tune. As I approached the counter, the cashier stood, and to my surprise, his face hardened as his eyes went from the customer back to me. Shit, he wasn't human. The cashier clamped his hands over his ears and began growling.

"Fucking quit," he demanded.

Turning to the customer, I stopped humming and addressed the idiot. "Go sit in your car for about twenty minutes, would you," the request tasted like acid on my tongue. That was the only drawback to a partial entrapment; you had to ask them to do things instead of ordering them. The effects of my vocal cords would last around an hour, though. Looking back at the cashier, I closed the distance and sat down my beer on the counter.

"Get out, Siren," he spat.

Pulling out my wallet, I nodded at the beer, and he dropped his hands from his ears, still glaring at me. "Good, now we can talk while you ring me up. I need to see your security footage."

"What the fuck makes you think I'm going to do that?"

"I could just gut your pathetic ass and figure it out myself while I walk out without paying for my beer."

"You walked in and tried pulling a Siren trick!"

78

"Because I don't have the time to deal with mortal fucks," I snapped, glaring at the male as I tried to place his species.

"That mortal fuck is my brother," he snarled.

My hand shot over the counter and grabbed him by the shirt, dragging him over the counter. "So you're a half-breed, whatever. Show me the fucking tapes."

"Let go and get out before I turn you into a fucking frog!"

"Tapes. Now," I snarled, bringing him nose to nose with me. Judging by the strong smell of coffee, he was a Warlock, weak as a mortal physically, but they were known to wield powerful magic. The start of a spell had barely left his lips when I smashed his face into the counter, the sound of his nose shattering giving me sick satisfaction. "Shut up and help me find my fucking sister," I snarled, letting go of his shirt. The later it got, the worse the itch in my throat became, and violence was calling me the way my kind's voice called ships to their death.

He groaned in pain and held his bleeding nose. "Just fucking ask next time," he said as he tossed a remote at me. "Fucking crazy-ass bitch."

His insult rolled off my back. Twelve thousand years of being this way had led to me hearing all kinds of insults. Any other time, I would have killed him for the pleasure of ridding the Earth of another male, but right now, Theia needed me. I walked around the counter to the screens and selected the menu, opening the recordings from the day Theia disappeared.

"You're still paying for the fucking beer," he said behind me as he held a rag to his nose.

"Just take the cash in my wallet," I said without looking away from the screen.

79

"What the fuck! You just walk around with a wad of hundreds in your wallet?"

"Take an extra hundred for the nose, I don't give a fuck," I snarled. The longer I spent in his presence, the more I longed to simply kill him. My eyes searched every car that appeared on the screen, pausing at every female I spotted who even remotely resembled my sister. Finally, I spotted her.

Her body was slumped over in the passenger seat of a Jeep, her head resting against the window. The shadows nearly obscured her from the camera's pathetic quality, but I spotted her when the Lycan had driven under the light as he was pulling in. Rage, hope, and relief all battled inside. She was alive; at least two days ago, she was still alive. Rewinding the footage, I paused and got a good look at the Lycan's face before looking at the license plate on the Jeep. When I caught up to them, I would murder the Lycan for daring to take my sister. I grabbed a slip of paper and wrote down the plate before grabbing my beer and walking out.

"Hey, what about my brother?" the Warlock called behind me.

"He'll come out of it eventually," was all I said as I made my way to the truck where Fin was waiting for me. Once I was in the truck, I shoved the slip of paper at him. "This is the Jeep they were driving."

"Good. What direction did they head when they left?"

"He pulled out and took a left as far as I could tell. We need to see if we can hack into the traffic cameras and track him that way."

80

Fin looked at me, then pulled out and took a left. "I'll see what I can do. For now, we need to get to my safehouse before sunrise. I'll use the daylight hours to try and track the vehicle through camera footage so that we might be able to find a way to head them off."

"That's the one drawback to you being a Vampire. You can't travel during the fucking day."

"It wasn't my choice to become this, but hey, why not make it my fault," he muttered.

"Shut up and drive." I didn't like the implication that his choice had been taken from him, not when I knew exactly what it was like to be forced into things. But those thoughts were better left to someone who cared.

Chapter 8

Ella…

As the sky was beginning to lighten, we arrived at his safehouse. Without saying a word, I climbed out of the truck and grabbed my bags. Approaching the door, I paused when I realized that there was a keypad lock. Fin up beside me and entered a code before the lock clicked. "After you," he said, gesturing for me to go in first.

As I walked into the safehouse, my eyes locked on Fin, the male who was my unlikely ally in this chaotic pursuit. Tall and lean, he exuded a quiet intensity that contradicted his human appearance. With tousled chestnut-brown hair and piercing hazel eyes that seemed to hold a depth of knowledge, he stood in stark contrast to my constant anger. Dressed in a dark jacket and jeans, Fin carried an air of mystery, with secrets hidden beneath his calm exterior.

After my quick assessment of him, I turned my attention to the interior of the safehouse. The curtains were all drawn, blocking out any light. I made my way to the couch and dropped my bags. "Where is a computer?" I asked, not wanting to waste any time.

82

"Here," he said, pulling a laptop out and setting it on the coffee table.

Flipping it open, I turned it on and sat on the edge of the couch. "What's the password?"

"What makes you think I'll tell you?" Fin quipped back in an amused tone.

"Vampire, I don't have time for your games," I grated out through clenched teeth, my patience teetering on thin ice.

"That is the password. Capital W, the rest lowercase, and replace all the L's with ones, no spaces. The question mark at the end is the special character. *WhatmakesyouthinkI11te11you?*"

"Are you fucking kidding me?" I demanded, glaring in disbelief.

His dark brows went up. "No, now, if you don't mind, I'm trying to listen for heartbeats. I'm not used to hearing my own, so I may need to clear the house room by room just to be safe. You can never be too safe."

My eyes narrowed as I glared at him, tilting his fucking head and stepping silently further into the house. "Vampire, do you know how to hack?" I knew I couldn't do it; computers and shit were Theia's thing.

"Yes, I do. I was wondering when you asked me for the password," he said, as he walked into the living room where I sat on the couch. "I can't hear any heartbeats in the house, but I'm also not used to hearing my own, so it's fucking me up."

"I'll clear the house. Hopefully, I'll find someone to kill," I said as I stood up.

"You have a wonderful outlook on life."

"Go to hell."

83

"Living it, Songbird."

"Would you quit," I snapped.

"You call me Leech and Vampire instead of using my name. Why am I not allowed to call you Acapella or Songbird?" he replied without looking up from the laptop he was typing on.

Gritting my teeth, I turned and walked away from him. He was as infuriating as dealing with both sisters rolled into one. If I were to stay in the same room with him for too long, I feared I'd kill him, and if I did that, I would be on my own. As much as I hated to admit, it even to myself, I needed his help, until Kassie found us.

I walked from room to room, hoping to find someone to release my anger on, but the house was empty. By the time I'd returned to the living room, Fin had footage pulled up on the laptop. "Have you found her?" I asked as I put my hands on the back of the couch and looked at the screen.

"Not yet. I just got access to the town, and now I need to narrow it down to the streets."

"Why do you have so many windows open?" I asked as I noticed the multiple tabs at the top of the screen.

"I needed to have a map of the town for the street names, as well as a map of all the gas stations pulled up to make it easier, or would you rather I just cross my fingers and hope I pick the right cameras to hack?"

"Whatever," I said, just restraining myself. The hope of finding a trail to my sister was the only thing keeping me in check. When this was all over, and I had both my sisters back, I would make Theia teach me how to hack. I was never going to be in this position again.

"Found them," Fin said as he pointed to the screen as he switched cameras until, finally, the Jeep pulled off onto a road, and Fin cursed. "There are no more cameras on that road." He opened another tab on the computer to a map. "It looks like a back road leading to the highway."

"Can you hack the highway?"

"If there are cameras on it, it's an old highway." He started plucking away at the keyboard without looking at his hands. After about twenty minutes of typing and cursing, he sighed and pushed the laptop back. "The bad news is I can't find any cameras on that highway. The good news is that we know they are heading north, and we can take a more direct route to get to that particular highway."

"How will we know which exit they got off on?"

He shook his head. "I really can't answer that. After we get some rest, we will head out. We can try to get to the next town known for Lycan activity and ask around tomorrow."

"Fucking worthless," I muttered as I straightened and walked toward the bathroom.

"Please tell me you're not going to turn your neck into a jack-o-lantern again," Fin said from behind me.

"Sure am. Unless you have a better idea," I turned to face him out of curiosity. He ran both hands through his hair and let out an exhausted breath. "That's what I thought," I said as I started to walk back toward the bathroom.

"I could bite you," he said faintly.

I froze as I processed what he'd said. Turning back around, I stood in the doorway of the bathroom. "Did you just ask if you could drink me?"

85

Closing his eyes, he shook his head before looking at the ceiling. "In a way, I suppose I did, but only because a Vampire's bite doesn't hurt after the initial breaking of the skin. I'd sink my teeth through your vocal cords, severing them, and drain enough blood to make you light-headed. That should do the trick, right? No need to stop your heart or cause yourself pain?"

Crossing my arms, I leaned against the door frame. "Why should you care about how much pain I feel?" My sisters had stopped trying to avert my self-mutilation decades ago. His concern struck an odd nerve, one I couldn't quite explain.

He gave me a look of confusion. "I just do. Do your sisters not try to dissuade you from this," he hesitated, "self-mutilation?"

"They gave up long ago, so should you." I wasn't about to tell him that I took comfort in the pain. The comfort stemmed from my choice instead of it being forced on me.

"What is the worst that could happen if we try my way?"

"I kill you for touching me," my heart was pounding in my chest. Would he try? Would he try to touch me? The last male whose lips had been on my flesh had been swallowed by flames and buried by the sea.

Hurt and anger flashed through his eyes. "I died a long time ago. If you ended my existence, it would be to set me free from this hell."

I rolled my eyes. "You are the most dramatic male I've ever encountered." I couldn't deny the relief his words had brought or the odd tinge of guilt.

"That's rich, coming from the person who carves open their throat every night."

86

"I don't carve, I slice. My cuts are always clean and precise." I was anything but sloppy.

"Bloody hell," he said in exasperation as he turned away from me.

My heart pounded in my ears. Was it possible he could ease my itch without sexual contact? Could he take the edge off for me without me losing consciousness and becoming completely vulnerable? "Fine." I'd lost my damn mind! Here I was, actually willing to let a male touch me to maintain a sense of control by staying conscious.

"What?" he asked, turning to face me.

"I said fine. We'll try your way, just this one time, but if it doesn't work, I'm ripping out your fangs and making myself some new jewelry." The thought of doing that anyway was also an appealing one; he was a male, after all.

"Fair enough," he agreed, his stance relaxed a bit. "Now, because of where your vocal cords are, I'll need you to lay down so I can bite vertically on them instead of horizontally."

"No," I responded, not liking the vulnerability of lying down while a male was touching me. Not that I liked the idea of a male touching me, but if it meant I didn't lose consciousness, then I was willing to deal with the momentary discomfort. Maybe.

He sighed and looked around the room momentarily before looking back at me. "How about you sit on the couch and lean your head back? I can stand behind the couch so that no other part of us touches?"

His ability to determine what made me so uncomfortable was irritating and refreshing. To have a male be considerate of me was not something I had ever encountered before, and it only

87

added to my distrust of him. "Then stand behind the couch already," I snapped, ready to get it over with.

He got up, walked around to the back of the couch, and waited for me to come take a seat. Double-stacking the cushions to make myself tall enough, I stretched and leaned my head over the back of the couch, trying to calm my nerves. "Make it quick; we don't have all night."

"I'll make it as quick as I can. Tap my arm when you want me to stop," Fin said as he walked up to one side of my head and placed his hands on the couch. I closed my eyes before I could watch him get any closer. The next thing I knew, his warm lips were on my throat as his sharp fangs easily pierced through my larynx with a slight pop. The itch in my throat died to a low hum as his fangs damaged my vocal cords.

Then he began to drink my blood, each pull sending tingles of pleasure through me, causing me to fist my hands on the couch cushion. I needed him to stop, but needed him to keep going all at the same time. How had I sunk this low to allow a male to touch me? How was I feeling pleasure from this? Was it part of a Vampire's bite? As my head began to spin, my hand shot up to grab his arm. His fangs immediately pulled out of my skin.

"Did I take too much? Are you hurt?" he questioned, an edge of panic in his voice.

I opened my eyes and let go of his arm as if he had burned me. Glancing at him, I sat forward on the couch, the room feeling wobbly as if I were drunk. It was stupid of him to ask me questions after he'd just damaged my vocal cords. Standing, I turned to face him while bracing myself on the couch. "*Bed*," I mouthed.

88

"Do you need my help? You look like you're going to fall over. Damn it, I took too much," he said, his face etched with concern. *I didn't care that he was concerned.* I rolled my eyes at his unwanted concern and I lurched away from the couch. My legs were leaden and uncoordinated, until I bumped against the wall, the cool surface a stark contrast to the heat that still lingered on my skin. When his hand reached out, I recoiled from him with a warning glare. His hands shot up, a gesture of surrender that did little to ease the heat coursing through me.

I stumbled into the bedroom and fumbled to shut the door before sliding to the floor, my back pressed against the solid wood. The world spun as I tried to reconcile the war raging within. No man's touch had ever given me pleasure, yet Finlay had unleashed a torrent of sensation that left me trembling. I despised him, every fiber of my being screaming in outrage, and yet, a perverse longing clawed at the edges of my consciousness, whispering insidious suggestions to crawl back in there and ask for him to keep going until I blacked out. *Fucking Vampire,* I cursed silently, the words a brittle shield against the unwanted desire to fade into sweet oblivion.

89

Chapter 9

Ella...

I woke to a crashing sound and jumped from the floor. As I flung open the door, I was greeted by the sight of the gas station attendant from last night and another male attacking Finlay. With a wicked smile, I surged from my room and launched myself at the attendant, but before I reached him, someone attacked me from the side. I was slammed into the wall by a large male. Twisting around, I sank my fingers into his throat and ripped out his jugular, blood spraying all over my face and running down my hand and arm.

Adrenaline pumped through my body as my attacker gargled and staggered back, his eyes wide. Launching forward, I knocked him to the ground. My hand moved with practiced speed, fingers finding the familiar grip of the knife tucked securely in my boot that I had failed to remove last night. In one quick motion, I sank it into his chest, the blade slipping neatly between his ribs and into his heart. Twisting my head around, I looked at the other two intruders to find Finlay relieving one attacker of his head while the attendant chanted. Smoke hissed from the

Vampire's body, and he roared in pain, his eyes latching onto the attendant as the room grew brighter.

A daylight spell. I pushed up from the floor and shot across the room at the attendant, locking my hand around his throat so tightly I cut his words off. "I'm going to enjoy killing you," I said before forcing him back against the wall and launching my fist into his jaw.

The brutal impact resonated up my arm, a symphony of exquisite agony. A beautiful, blossoming pain bloomed through my fist, a perverse testament to the force unleashed. I felt the satisfying crunch, the sickening give of bone and cartilage, as both my hand and the Warlock's jaw surrendered to the violence. His guttural cry was cut short, reduced to a strangled gasp, effectively rendering him unable to voice spells. Uncontrolled sounds of pain and panic came from his now misshapen jaw, blood running freely down his face.

His hands shot out toward my face, trying to claw at my eyes. Before I could do anything, Finlay's hands wrapped around the Warlock's wrist and pushed his hands away from me. I could feel the Vampire's body just behind me and went rigid as I held my target, unsure of what to do next as a male behind me brought back memories of long-ago torment.

"Shall I assist you in ridding this scum of his flesh?" Finlay asked from behind me, his voice vibrating into my spine in a way that was delicious, terrifying, and infuriating all at the same time.

"Help me rip his arms off. Once he passes out from blood loss and pain, we'll kill him," I responded, unsure of what else to do at the moment. The Vampire was stirring things in me that

91

didn't belong. Rage reared up as I thought of how he'd been burning only moments ago due to the Warlock in our grips. I tilted my head. "On second thought, he hurt you; this is your score to settle."

The Warlock's kick landed squarely on my shin, a sharp, brutal blow that sent a curse ripping from my throat. The next thing I knew, Finlay had ripped him from my grasp and hurled him across the room. He was on his prey in an instant at lightning-fast speed, a predator unleashed. The sounds that came from the Warlock were sounds of pure horror and pain as Finlay plunged his hand into his abdomen, ripping out a tangle of intestines. The sound of bones crunching as Finlay snarled, growling like some feral beast, and the sounds echoed through the large living room as he tore the male's ribs from his body. I stood frozen in place and watched Finlay rip the other male to shreds, even after his heart had stopped beating. Finally, with a final, savage motion, he ripped the Warlock's head from his body and sat atop his victim, panting and covered in blood.

"Feel better?" I asked, a little in awe at the beautiful violence that had just unfolded.

Without a word, Fin got to his feet, the head still in hand, with spinal fluid and blood dripping from it, and turned to face me. "Were you afraid of me?"

It took a moment for his question to register. "I've dismembered many opponents in my lifetime; why would watching someone else cause me fear?"

"Before that, when I stood behind you and held his hands away from you."

92

I narrowed my eyes at him. "It's you who should be afraid of me, Vampire."

He walked toward me and shoved the dismembered head into my chest. "You terrify me for reasons I can't even explain, female. And just so we're clear, I ripped this bastard apart because he touched you without your permission. Had we not been in a bar in public last night, I would have done the same to the Demon." With that, he walked to the bathroom and calmly shut the door behind him, leaving me alone with the three dismembered bodies.

A surge of anger coursed through me, a familiar shield against the tremor of fear that always lurked beneath the surface. I clung to the lie, the bravado that whispered I wasn't afraid of anything, even as the truth gnawed at me. I was a tangle of anxieties: the fear that my pain would be a constant, unyielding companion; the fear that the love I shared with my sisters, the very anchor of my existence, would one day fail to keep me afloat; and the even more terrifying prospect that I would become a burden, a weight that would pull them down. The deepest fear that clawed at my insides was that they would find someone else to live for, someone brighter, stronger, and who wasn't as broken as I was. The weight of it all pressed down on me, so I pivoted to a more familiar feeling.

Dropping the Warlock's head, I walked toward the bathroom. "Who's cleaning this shit up?" I yelled through the door, knowing he was in the shower but could still hear me.

The next thing I knew, the door was thrown open, and Fin stood there, water and blood trickling down his naked body. "I'll make a bloody phone call now if you don't mind; I was in the

93

middle of a shower." The reaction was instantaneous, a surge of adrenaline eclipsing reason. My fist, seemingly with a will of its own, shot forward and connected squarely with his face. The impact was sickeningly satisfying, a dull thud followed by the wet crunch of bone and cartilage. He stumbled backward, arms flailing for purchase, but the slick tile of the bathroom floor betrayed him. He landed hard, a crumpled heap of limbs and indignation.

"What the hell," he sputtered, his voice thick with pain and disbelief, as his hands instinctively flew to his now mangled nose. Blood bloomed between his fingers, a stark crimson stain against the white of his skin, painting a vivid picture of the chaos I had brought.

"Reflex," I said blankly before turning away and walking toward the steps. The need to get as far away from him as possible filled me. As soon as I reached the top of the steps, I opened the first window, letting what little morning light there was into the empty bedroom. *Chicken.* I wasn't ready to face the Vampire again, and I needed a shower. While I didn't mind being covered in blood and gore, washing it out after it dried was a pain in the ass.

Walking down the hall, I found the other bathroom and turned on the water. I climbed into the shower with my clothes on, seeing as they were also covered in blood, and began washing. Why had I given the Warlock to him? Had I wanted to allow him his revenge, or had I just wanted to get him away from me? Why hadn't I ripped the Warlock's head off and then Fin's? *No, not Fin, Leech.* Fin was too personal, which was the last thing I wanted from him. I cursed my broken fist, longing to punch the shower

94

wall. While it had been satisfying in the moment, I would spend the rest of the day and some of tomorrow healing the bones, unlike my vocal cords, which healed rapidly.

The fucking itch was already back. It always came back as my vocal cords healed. It wasn't as bad as last night, but it was still there. I wondered if maybe I needed my vocal cords completely ripped out. That had only happened once, and I don't remember how long the itch had been delayed. As the water washed over me and I stripped my soaked clothing, I wondered how much longer I would live to battle the itch. How many centuries could I make it before losing control again?

"Ella, the sun's up, you're up. I'm going to bed. Wake me if anything happens," the Vampire's voice called from down the hall.

"Doubtful," I muttered to myself. I didn't want to deal with him.

"Vampire hearing, Songbird."

I gritted my teeth at his response and continued to scrub my hair. I desperately wanted to relieve his head from his body, but the truth was painfully clear that I needed him. Not only did I not know how to hack cameras, I had no contacts or leads on the habits or dealings of Lycans. I also had no safehouses to stay in. I punched the wall with my good fist, feeling the bone fracture as the tile cracked. At least it was just a fracture; it would heal much faster than the other hand, a few hours, and I'd be using it again like nothing had happened.

When I was done washing the blood and gore from my body, I stepped out and wrapped myself in a towel. The sun was up far enough that the Vampire couldn't move about freely in the

95

house unless all the windows were covered. As I moved to my borrowed room, I was thankful the Vampire was nowhere to be seen. I dressed in clean clothes before returning upstairs to grab my dirty ones. Surely there was a washing machine in this house. If not, I'd at least already rinsed them in the shower. I could always wash and dry them the old-fashioned way.

I'd found the washing machine with the Vampire's clothes in it already and tossed mine in as well. By the time the clothes had finished washing and I was switching the damp clothes over into the dryer, exhaustion had started to sneak up on me. I had let the Leech drink enough blood to take me to the edge of passing out and then fought with some immortals. I should be ready for a good nap. The question was, could I sleep? How many millennia had it been since I'd slept without cutting my throat first?

Wandering into the room where I had 'slept' only a few hours ago, I sat on the bed. Would I be able to sleep? Did I trust the Vampire enough to sleep? That first night, I'd thought I was safe with him when I'd cut my vocal cords because I'd thought he was unbonded. It had been hard for me to close my eyes earlier, even after he'd drained enough to leave me light-headed and my vision fuzzy. Had I ever closed my eyes willingly with a male around? I didn't think so. I flopped back on the bed and closed my eyes. If I couldn't sleep, I could at least get some rest, right?

The sound of a phone ringing drew me out of the half-sleep I'd fallen into. Seeing Kassie's name, I answered, "Where the hell have you been?" Part of me felt relieved to hear her voice, but I didn't have time for relief.

"Where are you? Have you found her?" Kassie's panicked voice questioned, ignoring my question.

96

"Not yet. I'll text you the address of the safehouse we're at right now, but the bounty hunter I hired is a Vampire, so we can only cover so much ground at a time. Now tell me where the hell you've been. Is Clay's ass dead?" I put her on speakerphone as I walked down to the main floor, intending to look at the numbers outside on the mailbox.

Kassie sighed on the other end of the phone. "How did you figure it out?"

"He left his shit on the boat. If he's not dead, we'll use him to get Theia back first."

"We're *not* killing him."

"Fine, you don't have to watch."

"Ella, I'm not getting into this right now; our sister is missing."

"Welcome to the last week of my fucking life!" I opened the front door and looked at the mailbox, which had no numbers on it. "Fuck! There are no fucking numbers on the box! All I can tell you is a fucking street."

Kassie sighed again on the other end of the phone. "Do you have me on speakerphone?"

"Yes."

"I need you to open your maps on your phone; you know how to do that, right?"

"Fuck you, I'm not an idiot."

"Right, so turn on your location and stop acting like a cunt for five minutes."

"When I see you, I'm punching you in the fucking face for that," I said as I turned on my location.

97

"Love you too, Ella. Now set the destination to home and start from your location. That should give you an address. If not, you can take a screenshot and send it to me."

"Do you know how to hack street cameras?" I asked as I did what she said.

"No, why?" Her voice was confused.

"Are you bringing the monkey?"

"I'm not a monkey," Clay's voice sounded in the background.

"Do you have me on speaker with that fucking Swamp Ape?" I demanded.

"Yes, I have you on speakerphone with Clay. He's going to help get Theia back, and you're going to have to learn to live with it."

"Can you hack cameras, Swamp Fuck?" I addressed him with all the respect he deserved–none.

"So I'm allowed to talk to you now?" Clay's voice responded, thick with sarcasm and a Louisiana twang.

"Yes or no, motherfucker," I grated through gritted teeth.

"No, and I've never fornicated with your mother, so that term doesn't apply."

"Kassie, break his useless neck for me," I said as I walked back inside to see Fin standing in the doorway of a room, looking at me and the sunlight between us, causing my heart to hitch oddly.

"Not going to happen. Have you got an address for me yet or not?" Kassie's voice was firm, leaving no room to argue.

98

"If you bring me the phone, I can type it in," Fin said as he stepped to the edge of the shadows, protecting himself from the late morning rays and from me.

"Wait, another male is allowed to talk to her, but not me?" Clay's voice sounded from the phone in disbelief.

The Vampire's eyes hardened just before Kassie's voice responded to Clay, "It's a Vampire; that means he's not a male. We look at creatures without heartbeats as, well, safe. They are immune to our powers because they don't have a heartbeat," Kassie explained calmly to Clay.

"Don't sing; he's defective," I warned as I handed Fin the phone, ignoring how his fingers felt as they grazed mine, causing me to want to shiver, a touch I'd ignore.

"Not my fault, Songbird," Fin called me by what was apparently his new pet name for me, and it stuck its damn mark.

"Fuck you, Leech. Type the fucking address so my sister can get here."

"Defective? You have a heartbeat?" Kassie questioned.

"I've sent it. I'll print off the exits they may have taken off of the highway where we lost them. It would be more efficient to split up and look in several locations at once, as long as my employer agrees," Fin answered Kassie as he handed the phone back to me. His business mannerism was refreshing after our earlier exchange.

"The sooner we find Theia, the better," I replied, taking Kassie off speakerphone.

"You didn't answer my question, Leech. Do you have a heartbeat?" Kassie demanded in my ear.

99

"Yes, he does. He hates it, and I intend to solve his problem when this is all over. I'll see you in about an hour," I told Kassie. "And Clay, when my sister is done with you, I will remove your head from your body." I knew Fin could hear every word on either end of the phone, whether it was on speakerphone or not, but I didn't know how keen a Bigfoot's hearing was.

"Ella," Kassie snapped my name through the phone.

"I'd expect nothing less. I have a lot to make up for with you and your sisters. Just know that I'd die protecting my mate."

"Mate?" I repeated the word in a questioning tone.

"We'll see you soon," Kassie said in a hurried voice and hung up the phone.

"Did I hear you call him a Swamp Ape and a monkey?" Fin asked as he glared at the sunlight and worked his way around toward the kitchen. He sighed, "Ella, I know you hate me for being alive, but I can't exactly help you if I can't move around my own fucking safehouse. Please close the curtains."

"He's a Sasquatch," I responded as I closed the curtains. I only had to be alone with him for another hour before Kassie arrived. I was such a fucking weakling! I could easily kill him if he tried anything.

"He also said mate. Do you think your sister is his mate?"

I hesitated for a moment before glancing at him. "I'm not sure that's right. The first time we encountered him, we were hunting and singing. Kassie, specifically, was singing. Then Theia and I joined her, but it doesn't make any sense. He should have been driven crazy by all three of us singing."

"So, more than one Siren can entrap a single male at a time?" Fin asked as he walked through the kitchen and into a

100

small room off the side where a printer was set up with a built-in scanner.

"Yes, but they are so obsessed that they can't function without the Siren who sang to them being near them and at least humming to them occasionally. Without a constant supply of our magic, our victims would go crazy and die." Not that the three of us had ever done that before. If we fully entrapped anyone, we'd kill them soon after.

"He sounded perfectly fine to me. Are you sure it was the same creature? I didn't even know they could talk."

"He shape-shifts. Something none of us knew until just a few days ago."

"Interesting. I wonder if they are naturally immune to your songs? If it's the same one that was on the phone, it's the only thing that makes any sense."

"Why are you so interested?" I countered, suddenly feeling defensive.

"I'm a bounty hunter and an investigator. It's how I stay alive and get things done. If you don't want to answer my questions, go back to not talking to me. You seem to be pretty good at that anyway."

"Leech," I muttered, knowing he heard me. I walked back into the kitchen, looking at the living room full of blood-stained floorboards. The dismembered bodies appeared to be stuffed in trash bags.

"Thank you, Fin, for helping me find my sister even though I'm a pain in the ass to deal with. Oh, you're welcome, Ella; it's been a joy working with you despite the burning pain of each breath my shriveled lungs were forced to draw that first

101

night. Don't worry, I've adjusted, and the thundering pounding of my now beating heart isn't annoying at all." Fin's voice came from the office, laced heavily with sarcasm.

I turned to look at him and demanded, "Have you lost your mind?"

"Oh, I'm sorry, could you hear me? I had no idea you spoke Leech," he practically spat the last word.

Clenching my jaw, I chose to ignore him and instead asked, "How long until your cleaning crew gets here? These bodies are going to start to stink."

"I was going to put them in the freezer, but there isn't room for all of them. The cleaning crew will be here about an hour after dark."

"Could you get them here any quicker?"

"I'll see what I can do. I was trying to keep you from needing to interact with them. You don't strike me as a social person."

"Shut up and help me find some baking soda and vinegar. I need something to do, so I might as well clean this shit up." I'd be damned if his consideration was touching. Nope, not at all. Fuck him.

"I'm surprised you didn't ask for bleach," he said as he walked into the kitchen and started opening cabinets with me. "I found vinegar," he said, setting a gallon on the counter from under the sink.

"The cabinet also has a couple of large boxes of baking soda in it. I guess it's easier to keep the supplies on hand for cleaning up blood," I said as I pulled down a box from over the stove. Walking into the living room, I began sprinkling the baking

102

soda over the floor. "The cleaning crew can come in with bleach later. I don't want to smell it, and this will get a good amount up for them. I also highly doubt you are worried about the cops, seeing as you are employed by a company that practically owns them."

"Most immortals hold some level of control over the authorities, but it's always best to cover your ass," Fin said as he came in with the vinegar.

"It must be nice to have support. We've always just had to take care of ourselves." I took the vinegar from him and began splashing it over the baking soda. "We've always had to clean up our messes and only ever had each other to rely on. If the cops caught up with us, we had to take care of it ourselves because there are so many immortals who would rather see us dead. Not that we've had too much trouble covering our asses most of the time. We've been doing it for twelve thousand years."

"There was a time in my life when I would have heard that someone was over one hundred and been impressed. Then, I became immortal. I've met many who are a few thousand years old and more who are hundreds, but you are probably one of the oldest I've ever met. Yet I look at you, and you appear to be in your twenties."

"Twenty-five is when I set into immortality. I don't know what age most set into their immortality, but I feel ours was late." Why else would our mother and aunts have turned us away? If I thought there were any other reason, I'd be filled with more hatred, and I already had my sights set on Ares.

103

"Late? What makes you say that? You don't look any older than any of the other immortals I've met, other than the ones who were turned at later ages in an otherwise human life."

"It doesn't matter," I said as I watched the chemicals foam and bubble pink against the brown floorboards. He was right; most immortals appeared to be around twenty-something in their features. Did others come into their powers at an earlier age and stop aging? Why had my sisters and I not gotten our powers at an earlier age?

"I'll see if I can find a scrub brush so we can clean this up some more," Fin said, leaving me to my thoughts. Why his absence made me feel just a little more hollow was not a thought I wanted to dwell on, so I allowed myself to think of my mother a little longer.

Chapter 10

Ella...

We heard a knock on the door about an hour into silently cleaning the floor. Fin got up to answer it and stopped, eyeing the sunlight streaming through the window. "My sister would probably kill you on sight anyway," I said as I walked toward the door. What I said wasn't true; I was the only one of my sisters who hated males to such an extent that the mere idea of seeing them triggered a blood lust. I opened the door to find Kassie and Clay standing outside.

Kassie wrinkled her nose. "Why does it smell like vinegar?"

"It's to get rid of the blood, I'd say," Clay said from behind her.

"Come in. I'd be happy to clean up a little more," I responded as my stern gaze landed on the tall male with his messy brown hair, dark tan skin, almond eyes, high cheekbones, and broad frame. It made sense that he shape-shifted into an Indigenous creature of legend.

"Shut up and let us in," Kassie said, her face hardening.

105

I turned around, walked back into the living room, and watched as they closed the door. "Sleep with one eye open, Swamp Ape," I said as I went back to my cleaning.

"Seriously, Ella, can we not do this shit right now?" Kassie said as she stayed between us. The fact that she'd remained between him and me was the only reason I hadn't punched him already.

"At least I know it's not just me," Fin muttered.

"Shut up, Leech," I snapped.

"I owe you an apology," Clay began as he stepped around Kassie.

I threw my fist into his face, feeling a satisfying crunch as his nose broke. He staggered back, one hand on his nose, his other held up as if to say stop. "You fucking lied to all of us!" A shadow came from the side, and before I could fully turn, pain bloomed in my eye socket as Kassie's fist connected with it.

"Don't fucking touch him," she hissed as she threw another fist. I dodged this time, bending and shooting forward. I grabbed her around the waist and rushed her into the wall.

"He fucking lied to all of us!" I roared, immune to her fists connecting with my back. The next thing I knew, arms were around me, pulling me back. "Let go!" I roared.

I was turned away from my sister and then released. I spun to find myself face-to-face with Fin. "She's your sister. If I hurt her for hurting you, well, it wouldn't be good."

"Get the fuck out of the way, both of you," Kassie's voice came from behind him, and I glanced behind Fin to see Clay standing in front of Kassie.

106

"I should kill you for touching me," I said in a deadly quiet tone, my eyes locking with Fin's.

His hazel eyes didn't waver. "If I die by your hand, then so be it." I felt my stomach do a strange flip at his words and suppressed an odd shiver that wanted to creep its way up my spine.

"What the fuck is going on here?" demanded Kassie, shoving passed Clay. "I'm done fighting, Clay; let me talk to my sister."

"Apparently, I made his fucking heart start beating, but I can't find Theia without him, so I can't fucking kill him," I seethed.

"We've established that neither of us are happy about this. You are causing me to feel things that I shouldn't be feeling. Hell, I need to eat real food again. Do you know how fucking weird that is? You act like the only one inconvenienced here is you! I've never wanted to dismember a female for hitting another, but I fucking wanted to rip your sister's arm off, and you started the damn fight! Fucking control yourself! You put so much fucking effort into controlling your voice, acting like nothing is of interest, but then you lash out like a rabid animal!"

"You touch my mate, and I'll end you," Clay growled behind him, making my anger flare yet again.

"Clay," Kassie said in a pleading tone.

"Same sentiment, creature," Fin shot back, sparing a glance at the slightly larger male, making a smile want to tug at my lips, a smile I suppressed. The male had guts; I'd give him that.

107

"For crying out loud! Boys, excuse my sister and me for a moment. I think we need to figure some things out, and the two of you acting like we're possessions isn't helping," Kassie snapped.

I stepped up to Fin, nearly touching him. "Touch me again, and I'll rip off the offending arm." The smell of frankincense and myrrh filled my nostrils as I looked at him in those damn unwavering eyes of his.

"Fair enough, Female," Fin said as he stepped around me and walked back to his room.

"Why is that thing still alive?" I asked Kassie as I walked to the kitchen, nodding at Clay.

"Clay is still alive because I love him!" Kassie snapped from behind me.

"I gathered that much from how you act concerning him. I'm talking about how he heard all of us singing. At the very least, he should be going insane."

"We don't hear. We feel vibrations in our creature form," Clay said from the living room.

I turned and glared at him. "Good for you. Get the fuck out of my conversation."

"Calm down. It's his information to share, not mine. Just like anything about you or Theia isn't mine to share," Kassie spoke in an ancient tongue that only the two of us could comprehend.

"He keeps calling you his mate. Are you sure he didn't hear you?" I asked in the same language as I leaned against the kitchen counter.

108

Kassie wrapped her arms around herself and looked away from me before responding. *"He smelled me. That's why he charged us that first day."*

"He scents his mate like a wolf," I confirmed.

She nodded her head. *"What about you and the Leech? Are you all right?"*

"Why wouldn't I be?" I shot back, feeling defensive.

"I know how much you hate males, and he, well, he touched you," she said as she looked up at me with concerned eye: Kassie, ever the empathetic one.

"I'm managing. As soon as we find Ameltheia or his usefulness reaches an end, I'll dispose of him," I replied evenly.

"Are you going to be all right if Clay and I split up from the two of you? Following other leads?"

"The sooner we find Amaltheia, the sooner I can be rid of him."

"The sooner we find Ameltheia, the safer it is for her," Kassie countered.

"Don't ever insinuate that I'm not considering her safety. She is the only reason I contacted the male for help in the first place." My tone was deadly, with more emotion than usual slipping into it.

"I didn't mean it that way. I'm just as concerned about her as you are. Clay and I will get the information from your male and start following what leads he gives us while you wait for the sun to go down."

"He's not my male," I snapped through gritted teeth, my voice betraying more emotion than I intended—again.

109

"You know that language has its limits," Kassie responded in English with a sigh.

"Just get the information from him and go find our sister." The sadness in her eyes stung. We were both worried for Theia. She turned and left the kitchen, which I knew was hard for her. Had I been Theia, she would have hugged me, but I wasn't. I didn't hug my sisters often, but I wouldn't have stopped her. I was a little starved for physical comfort, but I'd never admit it. I'd never admit that I needed anything from anyone. I wouldn't allow myself to be that weak. "Clay, we need to talk to the Vampire. Be nice, please," Kassie said as she walked up to her *mate*.

"As long as he doesn't put his hands on you or your sisters, we won't have a problem."

"My sisters and I can take care of ourselves," Kassie responded before I could.

"Your ability to defend yourself isn't in question. I told you I'm a tribal creature, and as my mate, you and yours are now my tribe."

"Fuck you, Swamp Ape," I said as I walked into the living room and began cleaning up the mess from where I'd been trying to keep myself busy.

"That privilege belongs solely to your sister," he responded as he walked to the door Fin had gone through and knocked.

"Watch how you speak to her; she might punch you in the face again," Fin warned as he opened the door.

"Kassie warned me that I shouldn't even speak to her at all, but today I'm feeling a bit less cautious, seeing as a family member is in danger," Clay said, appearing to size up Fin.

110

Why was I using their names in my mind? They were males, creatures that deserve no respect. "Give them the leads, Leech," I said, emphasizing his parasitic nature with deliberate intent.

The Vampire sighed. "I'd planned on it." He looked Bigfoot up and down. "So you are a Sasquatch? I had no idea you had any form other than that of the ape-like creature."

"If you tell our secret to anyone, I'll find you and use your corpse to fertilize the swamps." the Sasquatch turned around and looked at Kassie with the papers in hand.

"I'm a hired gun. I know more secrets than most. I don't care to spread them as it would hinder my lifestyle," Fin, the Leech, said as he moved around the Bigfoot cautiously toward the office.

"We haven't opened any of the curtains. You shouldn't be burnt. I still need you," I said as I walked by him with the vinegar in hand.

"Nice to know my usefulness hasn't reached an end yet."

"As far as I can tell, that attitude doesn't go away," Bigfoot said to the Leech.

"That was clear from the start of my acquaintance with her." The Leech picked up the pages he'd printed off and handed them to Bigfoot. "I was able to gain access to the cameras and follow the vehicle to this road. This road leads to a highway, and neither of them has cameras. There are a few exits to search to find out where they have gone. I've marked the Lycan hot spots that should be searched."

111

"Kassie, when do you want to start looking?" The Sasquatch turned around and looked at my sister with the papers in hand.

Kassie looked at me. "I'd stay, but the sooner we find her, the better." The look on my sister's face was apologetic.

"I agree. The sooner we find her, the sooner we can be rid of the Leech, and the sooner Theia and I can talk you out of keeping your pet."

Kassie rolled her eyes. "Clay isn't a pet."

"We will start with the first exit Fin has marked. We can let them know what we find and how many spots we have checked," Clay said as he walked up to Kassie. Kassie gave me one more apologetic look before she and the Sasquatch turned and walked back out the door.

"With their help, we should be able to move twice as fast," the Leech said as he walked over to where I stood.

"They won't be much further ahead of us because of how close to dark it already is. If that dog has hurt my sister, I'm going to make his death extra painful," I said as I finished putting away the cleaning supplies.

"They will be at least four hours ahead of us unless it becomes overcast enough for me to get into the truck. The dark tint on the windows will protect me from the evening sun on a cloudy day."

"This is all great information if I were able to control the damn weather."

He sighed. "I was just telling you. I'll check the weather and see if there is a chance of us being able to leave any sooner."

112

"Finally, you say something almost useful." The Vampire let out a frustrated sigh as he walked out of the kitchen, and I felt a strange twinge of guilt that I would typically only feel with my sisters. The feeling fled almost as quickly as it had come. The abduction of my sisters over the last week must have made my emotions more out of control than I'd realized. The male deserved nothing from me but disdain. Leaving the kitchen, I went to the room I'd been in and started packing my belongings. If the weather were to permit, I wanted to be ready to leave right away instead of waiting until the sun was low enough for us to leave.

When I'd finished gathering my few belongings, the Leech knocked on my door frame with his phone in hand. "It looks like luck isn't on my side. It's supposed to be sunny for the next few days."

"We could always get you a beekeeper's outfit and finish this association much faster."

"I've tried that before, and I was unable to properly assist my employer in a fight, causing them serious harm, not to mention it draws quite a bit of attention from the mortals."

I turned to look at him. "If any mortal were to ask, I'd tell them you have mental problems and wish to pretend to be a beekeeper for the last week. As for a fight, I am more than capable of taking care of myself."

"I'm not doing it, so you may as well try to get some rest while you can," the Vampire said before turning around and leaving the room.

113

Chapter 11

Ella...

I was lying on top of the blankets, curled on my side facing the window, waiting for the sun to go down, and had at some point dozed off. A hand on my shoulder startled me out of my slumber, and I sprang to my feet and launched my fists blindly.

Fin dodged my fists. "Calm down, it's just me. It's time to go."

"Don't touch me," I spat out, enraged that he'd been able to dodge my fists.

He cocked a brow and looked at me. "Next time, I'll just bang on the door and order you out of the bed?"

"A quick knock on the door is enough," I told him as I got off the bed.

"It wasn't. I even said your name a few times, before I touched your shoulder. Luckily, I was prepared for you waking up swinging."

"Get out. I'm getting my things and we're leaving," I snapped, clearly frustrated.

"I already got your clothing out of the dryer. It's on the foot of your bed, so you can just put it in your bag, and we can leave," he said as he walked out of the room. My eyes narrowed at his back before I moved to gather my things. It didn't take me long to have everything in my bag and head out the door. I hated that he was ahead of me, already having everything loaded into the truck and ready to go. "I'll lock up while you get in the truck," he said as he stood by the door, waiting for me to leave. *Fucker.*

By the time I'd put my bag in the truck and gotten in the passenger seat, he was getting in on the driver's side. "Where are we headed first?" I asked, wanting to have something to think about other than wondering why I hadn't killed him yet.

"I was going to stop and get food to eat in the truck and then head to the second exit off that road. There is a Shifter club there where we might find some leads."

"What is with you and the Shifter bars?"

"Don't call this one a bar in front of any of the Shifters. As for your question, these are the places they hang out and brag about things. When you are in my business, this is where you get clients as well as how you track people."

"Are any of your leads going to not be at a bar?"

"I can't exactly check out the local coffee shops," he said with a glance out of the corner of his eye at me. "Not to mention, nearly every immortal I've ever met drinks and parties. The ones that don't typically don't need me." We fell silent as we drove. After about twenty minutes, we took an exit and drove another ten minutes through a small city, eventually arriving at the club I assumed he meant.

115

"Let's see what we can find out, shall we? I'll take the left while you take the right," he said as we got out of the truck.

We got to the door, and there was a bouncer with a rope behind him and a line waiting to get in. "This better not take all fucking night just to get in," I gritted out. I could feel the beat of the music from outside the building and knew it would be loud as fuck inside.

"It won't. I know Mav; he's a Bear," Fin said as he walked by the line, getting shitty looks and sarcastic remarks.

"Well, well, well. I suppose you have some business to take care of?" the Bear Shifter said to Fin as he crossed his massive arms and looked at us, sizing us up.

"Don't I always?" Fin asked coolly. The exchange wasn't friendly but civil.

The Bear looked at me. "What about you, sweetheart? You here for business or pleasure?"

I narrowed my eyes at him and tilted my head to the side. "If my business brings blood or rolling heads, then I'd call it both."

He narrowed his eyes. "Not a sweetheart, after all, are you?"

"Enough chatting, what's the price tonight?" Fin cut in, stepping slightly in front of me as if to stop me from killing the fucker.

"One thousand. Each."

Fin reached into his pocket, pulled out a wallet, and counted the bills. "Let's go," he said to me, and we walked in. "Most of them are Shifters here, so be careful what you say and do. There are a lot of mortals outside I'd rather not deal with."

116

"And here I thought you were worried about me."

"You made it very clear you don't want me to worry about you yesterday. I'll do my best to keep to your wishes as my employer." His tone was cold, and he didn't look at me. A strange feeling pulled inside me at his words. What the fuck was I feeling? Respect? For a male? No, it was regret that he wasn't giving me a fight; after all, I loved to fight.

I turned and walked away from him and pushed into the crowd. There were too many males for my comfort, but I knew I had to grit my teeth and get through it if I were going to find Theia. It looked like most of the people in the club were immortals. Then again, Fin had said this was a Shifter club. I just had to wonder how they kept the humans out. Maybe that was what the bouncing Bear was for at the door. Let the fucker shift around me, and I'd use him as a rug. The thought brought a small smile to my face.

I walked up to a female packing a drink in each hand back to her booth. "I need to find someone, and you just might be able to help me," I said, not beating around the bush. I was already over this place and its obnoxious music.

She looked me up and down and gave a seductive smile. "Come on over to our booth, and let's chat about it." I followed her to her booth, only to discover she was a Demon with a great ass but absolutely no useful information.

I went around the club like that for what felt like hours before Fin found me. "Let's go. I've got a lead."

"Really? Where are they?"

"Not that good of a lead, unfortunately, but I found out the locations of a few different Lycan houses two towns over. If we

117

head out now, we can check at least one of them and send your sister the information to check the other two," he said as he continued walking toward the door, his eyes darting around the club like he was on edge.

"What aren't you telling me?" I asked, half hoping there was a fight about to happen and not wanting to waste the time on one.

"This club always makes me nervous. They keep the beat where I can't hear the heartbeats of anyone. It's done on purpose because of Vampires. They don't like us here, but they tolerate us."

"It must be nice to be tolerated," I said as we walked out the door, only to be stopped by the Bear Shifter.

"There's an exit fee as well."

Fin went to pull out his wallet, but I locked my hand around his throat and pulled him down so that he was face to face with me, my fingers starting to break the skin of his throat. "How about this for an exit fee: I don't kill you for calling me sweetheart. I'm here to find someone who took my sister, and you're slowing me down—which means I have to waste even more time with this fucker." His eyes began to change, looking more animalistic, and his growl vibrated in my hand.

Fin put his hand around my wrist, making my breath hitch for only a second. "Let's not make a scene here with all these people watching. I have no problem paying him. After all, it's your money."

I let go of the Bear and turned to face Fin. "I told you what would happen if you touched me again."

118

"**R**ip off the arm later unless you can drive us where we need to go."

"Fucking leave, both of you," the Bear Shifter snarled. "And don't bring anyone to my club again unless you want to watch the sunrise before I rip your damn head off."

I ignored the Bear and walked toward the truck, seething and ready to kill Fin for touching me. The itch was roaring in my throat, and all I wanted to do was feel the hot rush of blood spilling from a body. I didn't care if that body was my own throat or someone else's. Climbing into the passenger seat, I decided that I would just wait until we got to the Lycan safehouse and find someone there to murder.

"WHAT THE FUCK WAS THAT?" Fin demanded as he got in, slamming the truck door.

"Shut up and drive," I said, leaning my head back as if I were going to take a nap. There was no fucking way I was taking a nap.

"**G**od damn it, Ella! I'm used to difficult clients, but that was stupid. You could have gotten us both killed! Hell, we probably both have a fucking price on our heads now! Mav isn't one to be fucked with!"

"**I**'m not one to be fucked with," I replied just before the truck door was wrenched open and Fin was hauled out of his seat by said Shifter.

I scrambled to get out of the truck as the Shifter's fist connected with Fin's face. A brutal exchange of blows followed, but Fin quickly recovered, deflecting the next strike and retaliating with his own powerful offense. I launched myself at the Shifter, scaling his back and locking my arm around his

119

throat, my legs instinctively securing around his torso. Fueled by adrenaline, I snarled, "Who's your sweetheart now, motherfucker?" He clawed at my arm, desperation etched in his struggle, but being the daughter of Ares, I was just as strong as he was. Fin regained his footing, landed a solid punch to the Shifter's gut. "Find your own teddy bear, Leech," I seethed as I clung to him with the tenacity of a rodeo rider and a bucking bull.

"He's shifting!"

A strange tingling sensation spread beneath my arm as fur started sprouting from his arm, and I felt the male's body beneath me contort. His muscles bunched and shifted, bones audibly cracking and reforming in a grotesque ballet, validating Fin's assertion that he was indeed shifting into his bear form. Sharp claws swiped at my side as the male, now a beast, desperately tried to dislodge me. Just as I thought I would be thrown off, Fin tackled the Bear with renewed speed, his hands clamping down on its jaws. The creature's neck snapped with a sickening twist, and the large Shifter collapsed back to the earth, still beneath my weight.

"Get," he panted, the command a huff of exhalation, "in the truck."

"And let you finish off this asshole? No, thanks," I retorted, a sarcastic edge to my voice, as I adjusted myself so that I was sitting on top of the Black Bear. My machete, annoyingly, remained in the truck. "I'll tell you what, you can get my machete out for me." Before I could say more, Fin's voice cut through the air, sharp and matter-of-fact.

"You're not killing him!" Fin exclaimed.

A skeptical eyebrow arched on my face. "Excuse me?"

120

He threw his hands on his hips, a dramatic gesture that was becoming his trademark. Looking up to the sky as if seeking divine counsel, he exasperatedly continued, "Ella, you can't kill my contacts just because they're assholes. Nearly every living creature is a fucking asshole! Not to mention," he added, his gaze dropping to meet mine with a hint of warning, "there are mortals present."

I muttered an indifferent, "Whatever," and started toward the truck, ready to leave the argument behind. "Oh, you've got some blood on your face," I pointed out, unable to resist the jab.

"Yeah, thanks for that," he snapped back, his tone laced with a potent cocktail of sarcasm and annoyance.

"He fractured my eye socket, too, if you were wondering. Fucking hurts."

"Pain is life," I recited, the phrase a well-worn mantra I'd repeated to my sisters countless times, the words automatic on my tongue. However, a primal urge surfaced—the urge to tear the Bear's head off, which grew a little stronger with every passing moment.

"No, it isn't," he said as he looked at me seriously. A silence descended, thick and unspoken, as we resumed the drive. Forty-five minutes later, the hum of the tires shifted as we veered onto a rough side road, finally coming to a halt. "Now would be a good time to arm ourselves with those wolfsbane-loaded weapons."

I met his eyes, a slow smile tugging at the corners of my lips as I retrieved a handgun from beneath my seat. "Like this one?" I asked, the glint of polished steel catching the dim light.

121

"Precisely," he replied, his focus unwavering. "Do you happen to have any more?"

"I already put one under your seat yesterday while you were asleep. I like to be prepared," I told him as I checked the magazine of my weapon.

"Okay, I'd rather not start shit here if we don't need to. This is a Lycan safehouse, and if there isn't anyone here, we may at least be able to find some clues. If there is someone here, we may be able to tell them that we've been hired to track a rogue wolf and get out without starting anything."

"Where's the fun in that?"

"Watching them leave or listen in on any calls they may make to warn whoever took your sister is the 'fun in that,' as you put it."

"It may be better if I stay in the truck now that I think of it. They'll know by my scent that I'm a Siren."

"That's another reason I stopped here," he said as he looked at me apologetically. "I was hoping you had a way to hide your scent."

A surge of self-loathing washed over me as the words escaped my lips. "The best I can do is hide in the back seat until you tell me it's safe, and if they smell me, just tell them the truth: you had a Siren for dinner last night." The blatant self-deprecation tasted like ash, and the look of disgust that immediately contorted his face mirrored my own revulsion. Good. I wanted him to hate that he drank my blood. I wanted him to hate me.

"Fine," his voice clipped, "get in the back then, and I'll let you know if it's safe." Once I was in the back and tucked down as

122

far as I could get, he began driving again. "It's an old farmhouse, not very big," he explained, the tension in his voice palpable. "It should be easy enough to search if there isn't anyone here. I don't see any vehicles, but that doesn't mean anything."

"Just get out and start looking to see if it's safe. You have eight bullets in the clip. They will slow them down more than normal if shit goes fun-ways."

"Fun-ways," he echoed, never looking back at me as he put the gun in his jacket pocket.

"Yes, others call it sideways; I call it fun-ways because it's more fun when it gets violent."

He shook his head before asking, "Has anyone ever told you that you're bloodthirsty?"

"That's rich, coming from a Vampire. Now get moving."

He got out of the truck, and I waited for what felt like an eternity before he came back out. "The house is empty, but I think they were here."

"How can you tell?" I asked, climbing out of my awkward position on the back floorboard.

"There is Siren blood inside," he stated.

I pushed past him and headed for the front door. "How do you know it's Siren blood? Even if it is, how can you be sure it's from my sister and not another Siren?"

As we entered, he was close, almost too close for comfort, his presence a constant shadow in my periphery. He knelt, his finger tracing a faint, reddish stain on the floor. "This area wasn't cleaned thoroughly," he remarked, his voice disturbingly calm. "And without chemicals, it seems." He paused, then, with a level of casualness that sent a chill down my spine, added, "To answer

123

your unspoken questions, yes, I tasted it. I'm quite confident this blood is related to you; the flavor profile is nearly identical."

"That's just fucking sick," I said.

He merely shrugged, his eyes holding a strange mixture of detachment and weariness. "I'm a Vampire," he explained, as if it were the most mundane thing. "It's not pleasant, but I utilize what I have to do my job, and believe me, sampling dried blood off the floor is hardly my idea of a good time."

"So what do we do now? You've confirmed that they were here. How do we figure out how long ago and where they went?" I asked, doing my best to ignore the fact that he had tasted my sister's blood and I was pissed about it.

"The blood is approximately three days old. Assuming they left shortly after this incident, they are at least that far ahead of us. As far as how to tell where they went from here, we have to turn this place upside down, thoroughly, to try to find any leads. I've already sent the locations of the other two Lycan safehouses to your other sister and her creature to check out. I will let them know what we've discovered here."

We began searching the house, looking for anything that might help us. Honestly, I had no idea what I was even looking for. I'd never had to do anything like this before. The only person my sisters and I had ever searched for was Ares, and he was a god who could just poof wherever the fuck he wanted. We had only caught up with the fucker a couple of times, only because he'd wanted us to.

"I have something on this pad. It's a good thing the Lycan is heavy-handed," Fin said as he scribbled on the paper with a pencil.

124

"Well, what have we got?" I demanded as I walked over to him.

"It's a list of items. It appears to be a spell of some kind. I'll have to reach out to my contacts and see if we can figure out what spell it is unless you think a Lycan puts Centaur hooves on a shopping list."

"Maybe he's looking for a chew toy," I muttered as I picked up the pad and read the rest of the items. "Gorgon scales, Centaur hooves, hibiscus pollen, crushed black lotus flower, three vials of weeping water, Phoenix feather, two black candles made from Ogre's ear wax, and thread. Where the fuck would he get all this stuff? Especially the Gorgon scales—I mean, he'd turn to stone."

"There is a market for everything. It just depends on how fresh the supplies need to be and where he has to take them," Fin said as he walked out the door.

As we climbed into his truck, I called Kassie and filled her in on the list. "How is he even supposed to get that stuff, and what happens when he does?" Kassie asked from the other end of the line.

"I asked the same questions. Apparently, there is a market for shit, whatever that means. I mean, I've heard of the black market, but we're not exactly familiar with any of it because we don't need to be."

"I guess if he's able to get the items on that list, we need to focus on what happens when he does," Kassie said.

"I'm working on it. I sent the list to the Witches at the agency. Hopefully, I'll have an answer soon enough," Fin told us.

125

"Next question: how do we figure out where they are going next?" Clay said on the other end of the phone.

"The only thing I can think to do is to keep checking the Lycan hot spots and hacking cameras when we find evidence that they have been in the area. We should also be looking at how to get the ingredients. If he's looking for them, we may just run into him," Fin said as he pulled out onto the main road.

"Where are we headed now?" I asked, wanting to let Kassie know.

"We're running out of dark, so I'm headed to one of my safehouses, and I'll start hacking cameras."

"We will check the other safehouses you sent us. We are about fifteen minutes from the first one. Let us know what you find," Kassie said.

"Be careful; I can only search for one sister at a time."

"Love you too, Ella," Kassie said before hanging up.

Chapter 12

Ella...

The next safehouse felt sterile, its furniture resembling a staged home for sale—pristine and impersonal. The air inside was stale, carrying a faint scent of dust and cleaning products. After confirming the space was empty, a heavy silence descended, broken only when Fin sank onto the couch and began typing away on the laptop. The soft tapping of the keys was the only sound, creating a rhythmic backdrop to our tension. He was still hunting for footage of the Jeep when his phone shattered the silence. We both startled at the sound.

"It's information on the spell," he announced, answering and putting it on speaker.

The voice on the other end came through cracked and digitized: "It took some digging, but it looks like a type of severing spell. Most of the time, two candles and a thread are used to cut ties between individuals, but the other ingredients suggest that the bond between the two parties is a magical one. It's not a Witch's spell though; more likely a Priestess's."

127

A foreign knot of fear tightened in my stomach. "Is it dangerous?" I pressed, wondering if my sister would be in danger if the Lycan were able to complete the spell.

The digitized voice on the other end of the line offered little comfort: "It shouldn't be, but obtaining the ingredients presents the real risk."

Fin drummed his fingers on his knee, disappointment etching lines around his eyes before asking, "Do you have a list of individuals who might be able to perform such a spell?"

"Regrettably, no. Like I said, it appears to be a Priestess spell. We don't have any with a location on record. They tend to move around regularly, making them harder to locate, and they don't like being associated with our company."

"I understand," Fin replied, his tone clipped. "Thank you for the information. Should you uncover anything else, please let me know immediately. This is a time-sensitive job."

"They always are with our organization." The line went dead, and Fin set the phone on the bare coffee table.

"I'm going to make something to eat while you keep looking for my sister," I said, pushing myself to my feet.

"Good luck with that. There isn't any food here," Fin said as he looked out the window, the curtains yet to be drawn. "We can always order something. I've had a client use a service called DoorDash. Do you know what that is?"

"I'm not an idiot," I snapped.

"Great, now that we've established that, I'd appreciate you ordering double of whatever you are planning on getting. While I don't need to eat real food, I like the way it tastes and feels. It's the only upside to what you've done to me."

128

"What I've done to you?" I couldn't help but retort, my frustration bubbling over. The nerve of him.

"Yes, you're the reason I'm breathing and have a heartbeat. The least you could do is order food for me, using my money, of course." I watched, dumbfounded, as he dug into his coat pocket and pulled out his wallet. "Here, use this card. I've got a lot of camera footage to review, so I'd appreciate the efficiency."

"Unbelievable," I muttered as I snatched his card and pulled out my phone. I was not about to admit I had never used DoorDash, so instead, I typed in 'pizza near me' into the search bar, then clicked on the first number that popped up. With a few aggravated taps on the screen, I'd ordered a supreme pizza with extra sauce and stuffed crust. Once the order was placed, I retrieved my bag. Methodically, I began to arrange my arsenal on the coffee table, the gleam of steel reflecting off the blades' surfaces with my whetstone in tow. Four throwing knives, two intimidating machetes, a pair of well-worn pocket knives, and a butterfly knife—each with a silent promise—now awaiting their purpose.

Fin's gaze lingered on the coffee table before he spoke. "Those are quality knives."

"They get the job done," I mumbled, already lost in the ritual of cleaning and sharpening. I couldn't bring myself to acknowledge, even silently, the pleasant warmth of his compliment. The rhythmic sound of the blade skating over the stone, usually soothing, felt hollow today. The metallic scrape was sharper, harsher, and it echoed in the quiet room, blending in with the sound of Fin's typing and clicking.

"I found them. It looks like they are headed toward Texas." Fin's voice held an edge of excitement, drawing me from the practiced motions that were falling short of their normal comfort.

Reaching for my phone, I quickly found Kassie's contact and dialed, putting the call on speaker. "Kassie, Fin spotted them on traffic cameras. They're headed toward Texas."

"We're changing direction now. What town are we headed for?" Clay's voice sounded in the background.

"Just a moment. I've had to backtrack the footage a few days because they are ahead of us," Fin said as he typed, the click-clack of the keyboard filling the brief silence. "It looks like they went to Lufkin yesterday."

"That doesn't exactly help us today," Kassie retorted, the impatience evident in her tone.

"I can't find them on any more traffic camera feeds. I'll keep looking. In the meantime, I'm also trying to track down the components for that spell list. Perhaps that will give us another angle. Unless, of course, you have any insight on acquiring those ingredients?"

Kassie's curt "Call us when you've got something. We're headed to Lufkin," was the last thing I heard before the line went dead.

"She's in a shit mood," I muttered, grabbing my whetstone and selecting another blade. The sharpening stone felt familiar in my hand, a poor attempt to ground myself against the rising tide of frustration. This situation was shit.

"So she's not always like this?" Fin asked as he kept clicking and scrolling.

130

"Normally, she says thank you and please and all that nice shit."

He sighed. "It was a rhetorical question. Due to our current situation, I had assumed that she would be in a bad mood."

"Just keep looking for something." I hated his understanding; it wasn't what males were supposed to be like. They were supposed to be self-centered and driven by desire. This male continued to be different, making things difficult for me. He was causing me to view him as more than just a bag of flesh. "If they've gone off the main roads again, then there isn't much I can do besides guessing where to pull footage from and hope we find them. I'm inputting routes into the GPS to see what the approximate time to reach the next location that has cameras for me to access. Then, I have to go through the process of accessing those cameras all over again. I think the best thing we can do is have your sister stop at all the gas stations she can and try to check the footage. Additionally, I've also got the access code and an address to the safehouse in the Lufkin area."

"I'm sure she would appreciate that. They will need to stop soon, seeing as they have been at it for nearly twenty-four hours now," I said, realizing that my sister had been covering way more ground than me. I let out a growl of frustration and flopped back in the chair I was sitting in. The damn itch was driving me crazy, the fucking Vampire was slowing me down, and I couldn't do the tech shit needed to track my sister.

"Hey," Fin said, drawing my attention, "We're going to find her."

"Damn right, we're going to find her," I retorted, the words sharp with a desperate urgency.

"I know you feel like I'm slowing you down; trust me, it's what I deal with already, but honestly, we should be able to catch up with them if I can figure out where they are going. Sending your other sister ahead of us is helping. We are working as a team, so we can cover more ground than I would be able to on my own."

Just then, a knock came at the door. "Fucking food's here," I muttered, rising to answer the door. My fingers instinctively closed around the familiar weight of my butterfly knife, the cool metal a strange comfort, reassuring in my grip. I knew garlic wouldn't deter a Vampire; they weren't allergic, but a petty hope lingered that he'd at least find it offensive. Pizza box in hand, I returned to the living room, dropping the delivery on the couch cushion furthest from him. Turning, I began clearing my blades from the coffee table, the scent of hot pizza mingling with the metallic tang of steel and sharpening oil. I transferred the box to the table, the rich aroma of garlic and melted cheese filling the air. "I hope you choke," I said as he reached for a slice.

He shrugged, his jaw tight with unspoken tension. "Then you would be without someone who can hack cameras, but sure, whatever."

I narrowed my eyes at him. His attitude was infuriating and somehow comforting at the same time. He was like the perfect mix of Theia and Kassie in his responses, and I hated it. Hated that I was finding any comfort in a male at all. I hated that I wasn't so sure I hated him.

132

I sat back down and ate my pizza before going back to sharpening. The itch was driving me mad! I needed a fucking drink, but I'd drunk all the beer I'd gotten the night before. Setting the blade down with a decisive clink, I turned to Fin. "Give me your keys," I demanded.

"What? Why?" His shock was evident in his voice.

"I want beer. Give me your keys so I can go get some."

He had an odd look on his face before he pulled the keys out of his pocket and tossed them on the coffee table. "Be careful, you did piss off a Bear earlier."

That was the look? He was worried about the Shifter coming after me? "I'll take his head if he tries anything. It's not like I haven't survived for twelve thousand years without a Vampire hitman." Why was I reassuring him? Fuck, I needed a damn drink. Snatching up the keys, a desperate plan began to take shape. Beer. A bathtub. That was the solution. One can, maybe two, and then I'd finally deal with this insatiable itch, consequences be damned. I'll cut the damn itch out. The bloodsucker could get bent.

Fin...

Ella was a walking storm of fury and recklessness, a constant source of my irritation. Whatever shadows clung to her past had clearly left deep scars. Despite my annoyance, I found myself consumed by thoughts of her, a persistent worry gnawing at me. Hell, I'd been living with a damn hard-on since I laid eyes on her, and my shower yesterday hadn't done much to take the edge off. The instant she left the safehouse, a simple errand for beer, my focus shattered. She was a damn disruption, a

133

captivating and infuriating distraction. Her return brought a wave of relief, a temporary reprieve from the chaos she embodied.

Her usual greeting, flat and devoid of warmth, held the faintest prickle of irritation. "Find anything?" she asked. Her tone was so characteristic that it often felt like anger was the only emotion she possessed. She presented a facade like she was made of unyielding stone, but beneath that impenetrable surface, I was starting to see a reservoir of emotion deeper than even she realized.

"No. We need to assume they have been staying in the same town for the past few days, which is good for our search. Hopefully, your other sister can locate them before they move on."

"Good," she replied, opening a bottle and beginning to pack away her blades. I suppose she was finished sharpening the already sharp steel.

I looked back at the computer and began typing while checking my messages. It seemed like the candles were easily found based on the list we'd discovered. The plants would also be straightforward to obtain. However, I was left wondering about the immortal body parts. The metallic scent of blood snagged my attention and jolted me from my thoughts. My heart raced as the sudden realization crashed over me like a wave: Ella was no longer in the room. Panic surged through me as I leaped off the couch and dashed to the bathroom.

As I burst through the door, Ella lay in the bathtub, her once-vibrant skin now ghostly pale against the stark white porcelain. Her throat was slit in a horrific gash. Blood poured from the wound in thick, pulsing streams, pooling in the bottom of the tub. She lay there, her body trembling, gasping for breath, though no sound emerged—only the frantic rhythm of her desperate inhalations. Each spurt of blood seemed to pulse in time with the frantic beat of my own heart, a grotesque reminder of the itch of the Siren call that plagued her.

"No, no, no," I cried out in desperation, collapsing to my knees as I pressed my hand against her bleeding throat. "Ella, damn it, we talked about this!" I raised my other wrist up to my mouth and bit down before forcing it over her mouth. "Drink!" Her eyes were already dimming, and she had lost consciousness before my wrist touched her lips. Even her immortality hadn't slowed the process enough for me to reach her in time. "Damn it," I cursed, falling back onto the floor, drenched in both her blood and my own. I closed my eyes, unable to bear the sight of her body struggling and ultimately failing to breathe. In a matter of two minutes, she'd stopped bleeding. It felt like an eternity.

The ringing of a phone caught my attention, pulling me from the chaos to the bathroom counter. I quickly wiped my hand off as best I could and picked up Ella's phone. "Hello?" I answered.

"Vampire? Where is my sister?" Kassie's voice echoed in my ear.

"In the bathtub, covered in both our blood," I replied, my voice laced with anger.

"Wait, both of your blood? What the fuck happened?"

"She slit her goddamn throat again, and I tried to force my blood down her before it was too late. But she fucking snuck in here, and I didn't reach her in time. That's what the fuck happened."

135

She was silent for a moment. "I still can't bear to watch it, and she's been doing it for longer than I can remember."

The empathy and sorrow in Kassie's voice were a sharp contrast to Ella. Ella was all anger or cold silence and efficacy. Yet now, she was too far away for me to reach, even as she lay there, just a foot from me, the edge of the tub the only thing between us.

"What the fuck are you talking about?" her male's voice sounded in the background.

"I'll explain later. Fin, right? Do you have any other leads for us now that we've made it?"

"No, I got distracted by your sister's little stunt. I'll get back to it and let you know when I find something." I struggled to suppress my anger in my voice, but it seeped through.

"Right, just place her bag in the bathroom so she can get cleaned up and dressed when she comes to in about six hours."

"Thanks," I responded, not knowing what else to say before ending the call. I set the phone down and started to wash the blood off my hands and arms in the sink before retrieving her bag. When I returned, I hesitated, contemplating whether to turn on the water and clean her up. The last time, she'd been naked, but now she was dressed in a T-shirt and cargo pants. If I ran the water, she would wake up cold and miserable. Yet, if I left the water off, she would wake up covered in itchy, irritating blood.

I had no right to strip and bathe her, not even to her undergarments. Hell, I had no right to lay a finger on her without her permission, regardless of my desire to simply hold her until she came back. The irrational part of me, the damn bonded part that seemed just on the edge of my control, was gripped by the

136

fear that she wouldn't come back. Meanwhile, the rational, logical part of me, that had guided me for the past five centuries, understood that as an immortal, she would recover without a trace or mark of her self-mutilation. So, I would sit here and wait it out.

137

Chapter 13

Ella...

After packing away all my knives except one, I took a long swig of my beer and walked to the bathroom. Fin was engrossed in his search for leads and was oblivious to my movements. In the bathroom, I downed the remainder of the beer and then sat in the tub, still dressed. The freshly sharpened blade felt cold against my skin as I drew it across my throat. Pain erupted as the steel sliced through my flesh, **a** sickening pop was the only sound from my severed vocal cords. The door crashed open, and Fin's face swam into view, stricken with distress. Blood roared in my ears, and darkness threatened to engulf me, his blurry figure reaching out just before I lost consciousness.

My unconscious mind took me back to my time with Helen—heated and passionate. It had been one of the rare moments in my life where I felt both intimate and relaxed with someone. Her touch was a flame, igniting my skin as her lips traced a path down my throat, a playful dance of nips and kisses along my collarbone and breasts. Her hand glided over my stomach, her fingers finding their way to my core with practiced ease. I surrendered to the sensation, my head falling back and my

138

eyes fluttering shut as she continued her descent, each caress building a crescendo of pleasure between my legs.

The gentle pressure of her hand was soon replaced by the intoxicating heat of her mouth. "Yes," I moaned, my voice trembling as her teeth grazed, then teased my clit before her tongue began its skilled work. "Fin!" I cried out as I climaxed, but in that instant, Helen's form morphed. Her delicate features twisted, changed, hardening into Fin's. His once-ordinary teeth elongated into sharp fangs that pierced my tender flesh, drinking deep as his mouth never ceased its torment, his tongue still exploring as he fed.

My heart hammered against my ribs, terror flooding my senses and stripping me of pleasure. Was this reality or a nightmare? I was paralyzed as Fin lifted his head from between my legs, his dark eyes locking onto mine. "Just doing my job, Songbird," he murmured, his voice a sensual whisper, before fading away, leaving me spiraling into blackness once more.

I jolted awake, sitting up and gasping, as I frantically looked around. Fin was glaring at me from outside the bathtub. He sat on the floor with the laptop in front of him. "We had a fucking deal," he said angrily.

"Get bent," I rasped, my voice hoarse and distorted, hardly above a whisper.

"Fuck you! It's past time you got off your goddamn high horse and lost the fucking chip on your shoulder! I've been here for the last five hours, waiting for you to wake up. Your selfish ass made my heart beat again, but then you go and stop yours! I hate this fucking bonded shit! I feel things that I shouldn't be feeling, and you're over there, carving out your throat and leaving

139

me to watch you bleed out and convulse in the fucking tub. Meanwhile, this supernatural bullshit makes me give a fuck! You're the one who needs to 'get bent.'" Fin shot to his feet and stormed out, leaving me in the tub, still covered in my own blood.

With a sigh, I got to my feet, pulling the shower curtain shut. My bloodied clothes landed in the tub with a soft thud. Dried blood flaking off like rusty powder, itching against my skin. I turned on the shower, letting the water wash the blood and the lingering scent of iron away. What had just happened? Had I really dreamed about Fin, about Helen? Had I dreamed about him taking Helen's place? The thought sent a shiver through me. I killed the water and stepped out, reaching for a towel. Instead of an empty counter, to my surprise, I found fresh clothes and a towel laid neatly folded, ready for me. Fin. He'd anticipated my needs, he'd taken care of it for me. A gesture that should have been comforting, but left me rooted to the spot, water beading on the cool tile floor, staring at the clothing. A torrent of uncertain, conflicting emotions threatened to drown me. Was I angry? Relieved? Confused? It was too much to process at once.

"We have about four hours left before we can leave. I'm going to get some sleep. Try not to carve out your throat in the meantime," Fin's voice was laced with barely suppressed anger as it filtered through the closed door.

Was it the bond making him do nice things for me? No, that didn't make sense. I'd seen mates be unapologetically dominant, controlling, and unrepentant in their cruelty. Fin was, above all, a professional. The way he treated me was part of his business aesthetic, a facet of his business persona. The bond wasn't making him kind—it was making him angry and blurring

140

his boundaries. It was making it hard for me to feel safe. My dream had been a stark reminder of what he wanted from me—my blood, my body, my money and resources. So why did a twinge of guilt keep creeping in, the same sensation I only felt when I was at odds with my sisters? Was the bond affecting me too? Or was it just my concern for Theia weighing on me?

A few hours passed while Fin slept. I stayed busy—packing everything, getting my clothes washed and dried. While he slept, I also went to the store and got some frozen food that would be easily microwaved, along with some coffee. There was no reason to keep allowing strangers to show up at whatever safehouse we were in when we could grab simple food to make. Not to mention, we were housebound for around ten hours every day while the sun was still too high for Fin. By the time he woke up, the aroma of freshly brewed coffee hung in the air, and everything was loaded into the truck.

"Ella, I think we need to talk," Fin said as he walked into the kitchen and got a cup of coffee. I looked at him. I didn't know what to say to him and wasn't sure I wanted to say anything. I still didn't know if I was safe with him or not. "I think the reason I get so upset when you cut your throat isn't just because of the bond. It's the smell of blood. It triggers my Vampire hunger. I'm caught between being in distress over seeing you that way and the urge to drink your blood."

"Is that it? If you're hungry, why not bite someone else while I bleed out? Problem solved."

He closed his eyes as his body tensed, the hum of electricity in the buttery light overhead seeming to echo the tension in his body. "It's not that simple. I don't just bite people. I

141

ask permission before touching anyone, something you seem to have missed in your oh-so-keen observations." Disdain dripped from his voice, his body humming with tension.

I shrugged. "I offered you my blood that first night. You told me you weren't a dog. I don't know what you expect me to do." Why was I being so nice to him? It didn't make sense. This wasn't me. Logic dictated he was a threat, a complication I couldn't afford. Yet, his words felt like anchors, dragging me toward a connection I desperately wanted to deny. "I'm going to eat and then I want to get going. I have a sister to find." His blatant honesty was making a mess of my head and emotions. Emotions were for the weak, and I wasn't weak. I couldn't afford to be. So why the hell was my head a mess, tangled with confusion and this stupid, undeniable pull toward him? I needed to shut it down. Logic. Instinct. Those were my weapons, and right now, they were failing me miserably against this unwanted, dangerous connection. I wanted to feel anything but this *damn* feeling.

His understanding dripped with sarcasm, each honeyed word a deliberate taunt."Gee, thanks for understanding. I knew you would; you're always on the same page." A shiver ran down my spine, not entirely unpleasant. A dangerous seed of something flickered within me, quickly smothered by a cold wave of self-disgust. It almost made me... like him? Wait, no. What the hell was I thinking? I needed to get my sister back and get the fuck away from this Vampire. My sister was the priority, not some bloodsucking parasite.

"Shut it, Leech," I snapped, grabbing a frozen breakfast out of the freezer and flopping it into the microwave. He made me uncomfortable in ways that I couldn't even explain. He had this unnerving way of getting under my skin, stirring up emotions I thought I'd longed buried and for whatever the reason, it was like I did care about his feelings, almost in the way I cared about my sisters'; and I didn't like it one bit. Gods only knew why I felt this odd sense of guilt over cutting my throat. The guilt had faded with my sisters long ago—they understood, didn't complain, a silent validation of understanding my way of coping. This fucker complained and wouldn't let it *go*. Why did his disapproval matter? Why did I care? He couldn't let it go. I hated him for making me question myself over something I have done since I escaped.

"**I** see you went to the store while I was asleep." Fin leaned against the counter, silhouetted against the dimming light filtering through the curtain over the sink.

"**W**hat else was I supposed to do? Sit there and watch you sleep?" The microwave beeped, signaling that my food was ready. I retrieved it and carried it over to the table, where my coffee sat. "I got two breakfast items and some lunch meat. I didn't feel like listening to you whine about wanting to taste the food. And for the love of the Gods, keep your fucking *foodgasm* to yourself this time. It's pathetic."

"**I** did that one time, just *once*, and you'll never let me hear the end of it, will you?" he groaned, the familiar exasperation lacing his voice.

"**N**ope," I mumbled back, mouth full. The eggs and potatoes were decent, but they were no match for Kassie or Theia's cooking. I missed my sisters. I was also sick of spending time with this fucker. I wasn't teasing him; I was being mean to

143

him. Why did I feel like I was lying to myself? The question gnawed at me, leaving a bitter taste alongside the breakfast, and it was such a foreign feeling.

"I'll get something to eat, and then we can leave. The sun should be low enough by then. You know I hate that I can't keep moving during the day, right?" he said, his voice tinged with guilt, the words hanging heavy in the air, a silent apology for the limitations his vampirism imposed on us both.

"Dead horse," I muttered, wanting nothing more than to shut down the conversation. Why was he so insistent on talking? I wanted it all to be over, to silence this damn persistent, gnawing itch in my throat, and find Theia. Exhausted didn't even begin to describe the state I was in, it would be an understatement. The self-inflicted wounds across my vocal cords offered only fleeting relief, taking the edge off, a meager distraction to offering crumbs to a starving man. The dark thought that I'd been contemplating ending my existence for good long before Theia had been taken wasn't too surprising. A selfish part of me still wanted to end my existence, or at least let go and entrap the world with my Siren's Call. If I did that, and I got rid of every male in existence, I would end the world. End every evil torment there was.

A cold shiver ran down my spine, a chilling echo of the power my sisters and I possessed. We were the ones who had ended civilizations before history knew to record itself, all with a little tune. The part that frightened me was that I had thought about it more than a few times. What kind of monster was I that toyed with the idea of ending the world by getting rid of all the males? A world without males meant the end of reproduction, leaving only the immortals to carry on and inherit the earth. The

144

idea of a world without males had always been an enticing one until I thought of the suffering the other females would go through who had males they loved. Kassie, I realized, now seemed to be one of those females.

"Are you all right?" Fin pulled me out of my thoughts.

"I'm fine." It was a familiar lie, a well-worn mask of deception I'd told my sisters and myself all too often. I stood and tossed the remnants of my microwave meal in the trash with a hollow thud. Refilling my coffee, I proceeded to walk into the living room. It was Fin's unnerving perceptiveness that had me on edge. My own sisters struggled to decipher me, yet he saw straight through me with an unnerving ease. Soon, we would be back on the road resuming our relentless search for Theia. That was comforting and unsettling because it meant I'd be crammed in the truck with him for who knew how long before we stopped to follow up on a lead or look for a new one. The list we'd found was only so helpful.

My mind kept drifting back to the dream I'd had—the dream of Fin giving me pleasure. I loathed the intrusion, the unwanted desire that seemed to mock my trauma. I hated it. My Siren abilities felt like a curse, the Vampire a looming threat in the next room, and the memories of the past a constant tormentor. The worst part of all was that there was nothing I could even do about it. The itch had already returned before he had even woken up. It had been so long since I'd felt pleasure that I wasn't even sure I remembered how it truly felt. Could I even experience it with a male after all I'd endured? My sisters had found pleasure with males, but they hadn't suffered the kind of abuse I had at the hands of males. Theia, perhaps, may understand more of my

145

suffering than Kassie, yet, I'd never really told them what all I'd gone through. I'd always kept the full extent of my suffering locked away. Why would I? What purpose would it serve for them to know of the torments of the past?

When my sisters found someone to satisfy them, how long did it take care of their itch? Did their itch ever entirely go away? Were Sirens even capable of being fully satisfied? Damn Poseidon for his absence, his knowledge lost to us, and damn our mother for tossing us out like trash, abandoning us. I felt a surge of raw, untamed anger and needed something to punch! I paced the living room, the anger and frustration echoing in each step.

"I know we have a lot of ground to cover, so if you want to drive, I can eat in the passenger seat. If you wreck my truck, I'll just add it to your bill," Fin said as he walked out of the kitchen, juggling a breakfast bowl in one hand and a travel mug in the other. His tone was enough to send a jolt of irritation through me. Without a word, I snatched the keys and walked out the door, hoping to find someone I could actually kill at the next stop.

Fin...

I watched Ella storm out of the safehouse, her frustration radiating off her in waves. The tension between us was thick, and I couldn't shake off the vivid image of her lying in that bathtub covered in blood. The bond was a relentless force, making me feel things I hadn't experienced in centuries. I could tell it was also pushing her limits, and I needed to find a way to navigate through the chaos.

A few minutes later, I gathered my thoughts and followed her outside. The truck's engine roared to life. I could sense the

146

internal struggle within her, and I knew that breaking down her walls would take time. The question was, did I want to break down those walls for me? Or was it the bond pushing me to do so, making me believe I was meant to fix her? Was I even capable of being her salvation, or was I just another male she'd grow to hate?

She was a beautiful chaos. There was a storm inside her, and I could almost feel its electricity, even through the walls she had put up. She masked it with anger and indifference, but I saw through it. I knew she wanted to protect herself, but I wondered if I was pushing her to let her guard down. Would she even allow it? Or would she hate me for trying? Her tactical and logical mind was intriguing, not to mention her unyielding loyalty to her sisters was admirable. She said she hated males, but still, she did these small things for me, like the breakfast bowl. Each one felt like a chink in her armor, but I couldn't decide if I was reading too much into it. Maybe she didn't want to be *completely* heartless.

As we hit the road, silence hung in the air. I took a deep breath, trying to find the right words to breach the barrier she had erected around herself. "Ella, I get it. The bond is messing with both of us, and I want to figure out how we can deal with it," I started cautiously.

She shot me a withering glance, her expression a mix of annoyance and uncertainty. "Deal with it? There's no dealing with this. It's just another damn thing on my plate. And as far as the bond goes, it's your bond, not mine."

"I know it's overwhelming, but shutting me out won't help. We're in this together, whether we like it or not." I knew she was right. The bond was mine, and I had no idea how to handle it,

147

but her words stung more than I cared to admit. She didn't see me as a partner—just a necessary evil in her quest for her sister.

Frustration flickered in her eyes, a fleeting desire to say more warring with a steely resolve. Her knuckles whitened as she clenched her fists, as a subtle sign of the tension coiling within her. The bond might have been mine, but the strain was written all over her face too. "Look, I don't know what you expect from me. This whole situation is a mess, and I know you can't control the damn bond. As far as 'together' goes, I only need you to help me find Theia."

"I don't expect anything more than cooperation. We need to find your sister, and we can't do that if we're at each other's throats." I wasn't asking for friendship, but I was asking for something—a truce, something. I wasn't about to let the bond control us, not when we were so close to finding Theia. I'd put up with her anger if it meant making some headway.

She remained silent for a moment before grumbling, "Fine, whatever. Just focus on finding Theia, and don't think this means we're friends."

I nodded, trying to keep my relief from showing too much. It was a small victory, but it was a victory nonetheless. She hadn't fully let her guard down, but it was a start. I hoped, in time, she might see that accepting support wasn't a weakness but a strength. The thought of helping her soften to the idea of relying on me... I couldn't deny the pull of wanting that. Even if it was just for this mission, it meant something.

148

Chapter 14

Ella...

After about an hour, we arrived in Lufkin. Kassie had sent a text saying she and Clay were back on the move, following Fin's leads and checking the local gas stations for any new information. Fin and I stopped at a bar. Thankfully, this one wasn't a Shifter bar—just an immortal one. When we reached the door, the bouncer narrowed his eyes on me. "This club is exclusive; you need an invitation."

"She's been exclusive longer than you've been undead," Fin said, stepping in front of me. "Normally, it's rude to talk about a lady's age, but she makes me feel young. I've been a member since 1557."

"In that case, go on in. You make a mess; you clean it up. Watch your backs in there; no one else will," the bouncer said, his tone bored, as if this was a rehearsed line. The fact that he hadn't scented me indicated he wasn't a Shifter or Vampire. Like me, he must have belonged to one of the immortals whose sense of smell was nearly human. Based on his size and the scent of leather as I passed him, I'd say he was a berserker.

149

"We're not just asking about the Lycan and your sister in here; we're asking about the list," Fin stated as he handed me a sheet of paper. I glanced down to see it was a copy of the ingredients the Lycan was after. "Don't get too far from me. This isn't the kind of bar you can afford to let your guard down in."

"I can handle myself," I snapped, not caring in the slightest that he gave a damn. Nope. In fact, I needed a fucking fight, a damn good one.

"I don't doubt that for a second," he replied, "But not many come to this bar alone, and I'd rather know that if you need my help—or if I need yours—we're close. Besides," he added, "you still need me to find her."

"I hate you." I hated him for not fighting me, for being right, and for making me feel confused all the damn time.

"Keep singing that tune. As long as I get paid, I can take the abuse." Before he could say another word, I drove my fist into his face, sending him staggering back. He wiped at the blood and chuckled as he looked at his hand. "Bloody hell. I offer my services, and this is the thanks I get?" He shook his head.

"Looks like you're not wanted," another man sneered, stepping beside me and slinging an arm over my shoulders. Without hesitation, I seized my grip on the male's arm and flipped him onto the floor. I planted my foot on his chest, kept my grip on his wrist, and tore his arm from his body. His horrified scream sent a sick thrill coursing through me.

I crouched beside him, the scent of grapefruit and mint hitting my nose—Merfolk. "No one asked for your opinion."

"You shouldn't have done that," a voice warned behind me.

150

I rose to my feet, a sadistic smile curving my lips. Two more males flanked the first on either side. "Are you three as weak as your friend here?" This was precisely what I needed, an outlet for my frustration Fin had been denying me by refusing to fight back.

"Fuck," Fin swore, the word barely out before the brawl erupted. The three of them spread out and charged, Fin shifting closer to me. He deflected a punch, while I dodged a kick and countered with a strike that would have shattered a human jaw. Fin landed a brutal right hook to one man's jaw, while I spun, my foot connecting with the third guy's stomach in a blow that sent him stumbling backward.

More than the initial three had joined the fight. At least five more males, the air thick with the scent of grapefruit and mint, surrounded Fin and me. They hesitated, their wary eyes assessing us. Fin and I moved back to back, as they charged, instinctively fighting in sync. Fin deflected a punch with his forearm while I drove my knee into another's ribs, following up with a sharp twist that snapped his neck. The remaining fighters circled, searching for an opening.

We countered the attacks, weaving between punches and kicks. Fin's speed and my agility complemented each other perfectly. While Fin handled his opponent, I unleashed a flurry of rapid strikes on mine. In moments, we had left every foolish opponent broken and bleeding. Breathing hard, I wiped a light spatter of blood from my face—remnants of the arm I'd torn off.

Silence settled over the bar, all eyes on us. "Well, there go our leads," Fin muttered, his back barely brushing mine. The

151

tingle of his nearness was comforting, knowing I wouldn't be attacked from behind, thanks to him.

"I need information. Anyone seen a Lycan dragging around a girl my size? Tattoos, blue and brown hair?" I addressed the crowd. A few mutters. A shuffle of feet. No one spoke up. "Fine. Next question—where can I get Gorgon scales?"

More silence followed, no one moving to answer or even attempting to get close to us. "I think we should just go. It doesn't look like anyone is going to answer any questions here."

"At least this stop was fun," I said as I turned and began walking toward the door, only to have Fin step in front of me, blocking my path.

"We should probably take the back door, you know, because of the blood and all," he said, gesturing at me.

"That's why I don't do nice clothes," I said, scanning for another exit.

"Back door's over there,' a female said, pointing to the exit.

Fin and I strode across the bar, the patrons instinctively stepping aside as we passed. We stepped into the night, the door swinging shut behind us, and Fin broke the silence with a low chuckle. "What?" I asked, my curiosity piqued.

"I was merely reflecting on how you tore that male's arm from his body. It was bloody brilliant."

"Bloody brilliant?" I repeated with a raised brow.

"The way you moved, flipping him over your shoulder and onto the ground, was beautiful and fluid. But when you ripped off his arm? That was brilliant." His dark eyes glinted

152

under the streetlamp's dim glow as we crossed the lot toward his truck.

"Brilliant. Not a word I have ever heard used for me." My sisters had called me lethal, efficient, and unhinged but never brilliant. The word felt... nice.

"Then you have been in the company of fools for far too long," he said, his smile unwavering, holding the passenger door open.

"Thank you," I murmured, the sound barely audible. For the first time in my long existence, I found myself at a loss, unsure how to react. Here in front of me, was a male, covered in blood, yet he was smiling at me. It wasn't the kind of a smile I was accustomed to—the twisted smiles, ones of ill intent. Instead, this was a smile of genuine warmth, the kind a friend might offer. My heart was pounding as my body flooded with feelings I didn't quite understand. The familiar, gnawing itch in my throat intensified, demanding to be quenched. Could he be the one to feed that itch?

His smile faltered as he looked at me, replaced by a look of concern. "Are you all right? What's wrong?"

His words snapped me out of my trance. "I... I think we need to change before we go anywhere else to look for leads."

"Right, we are covered in blood," he said as he let go of my truck door and stepped back, all traces of his smile gone. I hated to see it go. Why? Why did I care? "There is a company safehouse about ten minutes from here. We'll go there and get cleaned up before we head back out." He walked around the truck and got in. The engine roared to life, and we pulled out of the bar

153

parking lot, the moment lost. An odd twinge of pain struck my chest.

"Bite me," I said, breaking the silence after about five minutes of driving.

"I thought we were past this, at least for a while. What did I do now?"

"No, I need your teeth in my throat. When we get to the safehouse. The fight—it made the itch worse." It wasn't entirely a lie.

"Oh. I apologize for the misunderstanding. I'll gladly assist in relieving you of this discomfort."

He reverted to a clinical and distant demeanor, a professional once again. I should have been relieved, but I wasn't. Did I want him to fight with me? Was this because I missed my sisters? What was wrong with me? I leaned my head against the cool glass of the window and took in the darkness as we drove. It was only a few more minutes before we reached the safehouse he'd talked about.

I followed him to the door and waited with my bag in hand while he punched in the code. He stepped through the door and tilted his head, listening. "I only hear our hearts, so it should be safe. If you want to get cleaned up first, I'll make sure the house is clear. The less time we spend here, the more time we can spend looking for your sister."

"Sure thing, just as soon as I find the bathroom," I said in my dry tone.

He sighed. "On the table right there. There is a layout of the house. The company does this for all of their properties. I

154

don't do that with my own homes because they are mine and mine alone."

"Fair enough," I said, picking up the paper and quickly scanned the floor plan. It was a two-bed, two-bath with an eat-in kitchen, a living room, and a laundry room. I made my way to the bedroom to the left of the entrance and into the connected bathroom. Stripping my shirt over my head, I turned on the hot water in the sink and glanced around to find a basket of rags and towels under the sink. It took only a few minutes for me to clean the blood off my face and arms and put on a fresh shirt. I changed my pants, pulling on dark cargo pants and a fitted T-shirt. I'd learned a long time ago not to give my opponents loose fabric to grab onto.

Walking out of the bathroom, I found Fin buttoning up a new shirt in the living room. He'd gotten far less blood on him than I had, probably due to him not dismembering anyone as I had. Only one had lost an arm. The others had crumpled under the force of my fists, knees, elbows, and kicks. Fractured ribs, snapped joints. Damage calculated for efficiency. I hadn't lingered long enough to watch them struggle to breathe. Fin looked up at me. "If you'd like to sit on the couch as before, I won't take as much as last time. We need you to be able to function. Assuming you still want me to." He sounded unsure as he dropped his hands from the last button.

I swallowed and sat on the couch, leaning my head back and closing my eyes. "I need you to damage my vocal cords. Just enough to stop the damn itch."

"Right," he said, and I heard him move behind the sofa. The smell of frankincense filled my nostrils, and I felt his hands

155

settle on either side of my shoulders, putting pressure on the couch. I was hyper-aware of everything—his proximity, the weight of his touch, the way the air seemed to thrum with the tension between us. "I'm going to bite you now," he said. "Don't hit me."

His breath fanned my throat for a moment before I felt the sharp pinch of his fangs break through the tender skin at my neck, sliding through muscle, cartilage, and tendon with ease. The initial sting was sharp but fleeting, quickly replaced by the burn of his fangs sinking deep. His lips pressed against my skin, hot and wet, and I felt him sink further, a quiet, consuming pressure. My fingers slipped into his hair of their own accord. He tensed for just a beat, but the firm pressure of my hand on his head stilled him. My body hummed as he sucked at the wound he'd created, his fangs still buried in my neck. Two, three, then four long draws before his fangs retracted, and his tongue flicked quickly over the wounds, sealing them.

Disappointment flooded my body, and I held his head for a moment longer, reluctant to break the connection.

"Ella, I need you to let go," his voice strained.

My eyes shot open, and I jerked my hand away. I shot to my feet and staggered for a moment, the blood loss causing me to feel light-headed. Taking a steadying breath, I turned to face him. He stood so still behind the couch that he could've been a statue. "Thank you," I mouthed, then turned and walked to where I'd dropped my bag on the floor.

"Right, we should be going," he said from behind me. I opened the door and walked out, leaving it open behind me. Tossing my bag in the back seat, I climbed into the truck and sat

156

silently, staring out into the darkness again. "The next place is a Witch's shop. The owner might be able to give us some leads on where to get the things from that list, and if we're lucky, they've stopped there looking for things as well," Fin said as he got in the truck and turned over the engine.

By the time we arrived at the Witch's shop, my vocal cords had healed enough to leave me with a scratchy voice, similar to that of a mortal suffering from a severe case of bronchitis. As we entered the store, I took in the dim lighting and cluttered shelves. There were jars of dried herbs, books, candles, and other items of spellwork filling every space in the small shop.

"What brings you to my shop?" a slender female with flawless ebony skin asked as she stepped around the counter, her gaze sweeping the room. "Do I need to close early?"

"We were hoping you could assist us with a list of items," Fin said, handing her the slip of paper.

Her rich brown eyes flashed almost purple as she scanned the list. Both her eyes and the scent of peppermint mocha as she'd neared, were evidence of her being a Priestess. "This is quite the list. The lotus and hibiscus can be found here, but for the others, you'll need to do some traveling." She looked between us before continuing, "Some of these items will be dangerous to obtain, while others are simple purchases. This is a more powerful spell than I'm accustomed to seeing from beings of your kind."

"I'm not looking to acquire the items but rather to find out where to get them," Fin said carefully.

The female tilted her head, her slender, black-tipped fingers brushing the necklace around her neck, her eyes flashing with purple once more. "Shall we consult with the bones to find

157

your quarry, Vampire?" She tilted her head in the other direction and looked at me. "You've employed him for this job. I see you've paid in blood tonight; your aura still bears the mark of his bite over your vocal cords. Interesting."

I narrowed my eyes, wondering how strong my voice would be if I told her to go fuck herself. "Bones, Priestess," I said instead. My voice was indeed weak and raspy.

She smiled. "Very well, Siren." She raised a finger, muttered a few words, and the locks on the door slid into place, the sign flipping with a loud flap against the glass. "Right this way," she said, walking to a door behind the counter. We walked into a room with more jars of various things lining the walls, a square table with four chairs, a cauldron in the corner, and a wooden box on the table.

She opened the box, and a rattle greeted us, followed by a hiss. "Miss Nia has company, say hello." A diamondback rattlesnake slithered out of the box and stretched its odd-looking body across the table before coiling up and raising its head, almost like a puppet on a string. As I looked at its distorted face, I realized that the creature was not only dead but had no bones in its body. "They want me to ask your bones for help, my pet. Are they worthy?"

The snake turned its slightly sunken head toward me, its black tongue flicking out to taste the air and then to Fin before settling itself into a bundle of coils, blinking its unnatural eyes at the Priestess. "Very well then, we have his permission. Sit, and we will proceed," she said as she placed a serving platter on the table, a small bowl of bones, and other random objects. She cast her dark eyes toward us and waited for us to sit.

158

I watched as she rattled the items in the bowl before scattering them on the platter. The snake slithered its body around the platter and lifted its head to look at the pattern made there before turning its head to the Priestess, its dark tongue tasting the air once more. "I see," she said as though she were talking to the snake. "You are not as behind on your journey as you think," she said as she cast her eyes at me. "The changes you have long feared are coming true, and you will not be able to stop them. However, this doesn't mean the loss you think. This journey will lead you to a battle like no other."

She picked at the items, lifting some and presenting them to the snake. I watched carefully and saw only the flickering of its tongue. "Of course, that makes sense." She did this a few more times before looking back at us. "Dust and desert, followed by winds and rain. Hooves and tears, you'll reach your end. Travel west and north, stick to your current course, and you will reach the trail's end with blood and loss left in your wake."

She turned back to the snake and watched as it turned to the bones and struck the plate, causing the items to bounce and dance to new positions once more. "You will find your next lead in an Elf's shop. The name she bears is…" she tilted her head as she looked at the snake, who flicked his tongue at her again, "Lola." The snake slithered back into the box as soon as the name left her lips. "Now for payment, Vampire, I'll take three vials of your blood." The Priestess stood, opened a cabinet behind her, and placed three empty vials, a tourniquet, and a needle still in the packaging on the table.

159

Fin rolled up his sleeve as he looked at me and then back to the Priestess. "Do I want to know what you're going to do with it?"

She shrugged. "You never know when you need such a thing. Everything has a price."

"How do we find Lola?" I demanded, my voice still raspy.

"Look for Lola's Place. It may be named Lola's Shop, but it's the establishment's name. If you want more from me, then you'll have to give some of your song, which you can't for a while yet. Granted, the healing of your aura is impressive, even with all the scar tissue there."

"Auras have scar tissue?" Fin asked, removing the needle from his arm and curling it with a cotton swab I hadn't seen him pick up.

"Not all. The aura is made of energy. It only truly heals if the host truly heals." She looked at me. "If the host allows it to heal."

"I suppose immortality will always have something new to learn," Fin said as he stepped toward me. "Shall I see about locating Lola's while you drive?"

Chapter 15

Ella...

Fin had put the address for the next safehouse into my phone so he could focus on searching for this... Lola's Place the Priestess had told us about. Climbing into the truck, I put my phone on the dash mount he had installed before buckling my seatbelt.

Fin cursed from the passenger seat only seconds after his door had closed. "Of course, she'd give us a name that's all over Texas."

"Then we search them all. I'll call Kassie," I said, my voice almost normal.

"I'll try to narrow it down first. I doubt it's the restaurant chain." He returned to his phone, typing and scrolling. "I'll reach out to the company and check if any immortal shops go by Lola's."

"Just do it." I needed to find my sister as soon as possible. It had already been four days. What had happened to her during that time? I began driving toward the safehouse, wondering what conditions my sister was being kept in. The Lycan safehouse we'd found had been decent enough.

161

We were nearly at the safehouse when Fin broke the silence. "I've narrowed it down to about a dozen places. I've already sent them to Kassie and Clay."

"Good, they can keep searching while we sleep. The sun will rise soon."

"I'll keep checking the cameras and check in with my contacts to see if there are any other leads." He didn't look up as he frowned at his phone.

My throat burned as I watched him from the corner of my eye. I needed him to bite me again. The itch was a living, breathing thing that couldn't be killed. A small, sick part of me liked the way Fin's fangs felt in my throat, how his hot, soft lips felt pressed against my skin. No, I didn't like it—I liked the relief his bite brought. We were silent as we headed to the safehouse.

When we got there, Fin went first and opened the door, tilting his head and listening. "All clear."

"Boring." I brushed past him with my bags, scanning the living room. It was like any other living room: four walls, a couch, and a coffee table. There was a hallway to the left that looked like it veered into a kitchen, so I turned right. The first door I came to led to a bedroom, and I wasted no time dropping my bags at the foot of the bed, staking my claim. My gaze shot to the duffel that held the bulk of my knives. I could always just take care of the itch myself.

Fin cleared his throat, leaning against the doorway with his arms crossed over his fit chest. I turned to look at him. "I'm waiting on a response from the agency about where we can locate the items on the list still. If you would like, I can try to teach you how I hack the cameras."

162

I blinked at him. "If you teach me how to hack them, what will you do?" I'd made it clear that his usefulness didn't extend beyond his ability to hack cameras. Was he looking to distance himself from me? To find a way out of the contract?

He shrugged. "I'd search traffic cameras you weren't covering, doubling the virtual ground."

"Maybe later. I think I'll order something for dinner first. Chicken Alfredo from that pizza joint—once I remember its name." Why was I telling him this? Why had I spoken so much? Why was I worried about him teaching me to hack cameras? It would be one less thing to depend on him for.

He furrowed his brows in confusion. "I think it's Pizza Hut?" One of his dark brows arched in question as he added, "Shouldn't you be the one telling me the names of restaurants? I haven't eaten real food in the last five hundred years."

"Bite me," I shot back, narrowing my eyes. "My sisters deal with mortals more than I do."

He gave me a sad smile, his shadowed eyes gleaming in the soft light. "Just think, after we find Theia, you can order her something and surprise her."

"She'd think I'd lost my mind." Why was he so kind? Males weren't supposed to be this… caring.

"Because you ordered dinner for once?" One of his dark brows arched on his angular face.

"Because I don't do things like that for my sisters. Not really." I looked around the room, though I didn't know what for. "We take care of ourselves, but we take care of each other too. I'm the strong one, Kassie's the sensitive one, and Theia…" I swallowed, thinking about how my sister and I had argued, about

163

everything that led up to Kassie, then Theia, being taken away from me. "Theia is the funny one." The description fell short of who she really was. Theia was full of sarcasm and energy. She had an understanding of Kassie that I lacked, and a depth of pain she hid behind her beautiful face.

"Then I should get along with her wonderfully." He stood up from where he leaned in the doorframe. "I'm going to the living room to start searching. If you need anything, just let me know." He turned to leave but paused, looking back at me with pleading eyes that stood out in his sharply defined face. "Please don't, you know... unless you have to." With that, he left—he couldn't even say it.

Sighing heavily, I pulled out my phone and sat on the bed. Within moments, I'd ordered enough food for the two of us, which felt weird. Why did I care if I ordered enough for both of us? Why had I bought him food yesterday? Shaking my head, I grabbed my bag of clothes and walked across the hall to the bathroom I had seen. It would take me less time to shower than for the food to arrive, so I did.

When I finished, I dressed and made my way to the living room to wait for the delivery. Fin glanced up at me from the computer, then back to his search. Though his look had been quick, it was long enough for me to catch the relief in his dark eyes. "No luck with the traffic cameras yet, but the agency gave me some feedback to check out regarding the ingredients."

I didn't have to wait long before our food arrived. Fin watched the door from his shadowed spot on the couch as I took the food from the human male who delivered it. I'd not given the male a chance to say thank you as I shut the door in his face,

164

walked back to the coffee table, and set it down. "I got enough for both of us, so you don't need to bitch about being hungry." Yeah, because that was why I'd ordered him food—not because part of me was starting to care about him.

He tilted his head and looked at me. "It's not the same as the hunger I feel for blood. The blood is something I can't deny. I just enjoy the taste of food, and a small part of my stomach grumbles in demand."

"Eat, don't eat. I don't give a fuck." I refused to admit that his explanation was comforting, if only because it broke up the silence. I was used to living with two sisters, and the three of us were not quiet.

"I wasn't trying to start a fight, just making conversation." His voice carried the weight of exhaustion as he pushed himself off the couch and headed into the kitchen. When he returned, he held two forks and a bottle of wine. "No clue when I left this here, but if you like wine, we've got wine. I was hoping for beer."

"I've lived in places without beer, so wine works," I said, reaching for the bottle. A dry red. "Got a corkscrew?"

"There should be one in the kitchen. Let me check."

I watched as he disappeared into the kitchen. He was being decent, and I was being a bitch. But that was how I was with my sisters, too. When he returned, he flashed a half-smile and held up the corkscrew. "Found one. Maybe on the way to the next safehouse, we grab beer instead of wine. I hate the stuff."

"Why?" The question slipped out before I could stop it. Why the hell was I keeping this conversation going? Why did I care?

165

"It was her favorite drink, Colette." He sat on the couch and picked up his pan of pasta. "I found out later that she preferred it because she could mix blood into it and no one would know. It was also the wine that made it easier for me to make that bad decision the first time. I knew she was the king's lover—everyone did. Once I'd made the mistake of taking her to my bed the first time, it was easier for her to convince me over and over again, always plying me with wine. Honestly, I think I stayed inebriated for two weeks because of her."

He shook his head, his gaze drifting toward the ceiling before he continued. "When they finally caught us, we were in the king's wine cellar. The guards beat me unconscious and threw me into a cell. Later, Colette visited me there—with more wine. When I asked for water, she said the wine would calm my nerves since the king planned to hang me at dawn. I drank it, its sweetness laced with a metallic bite, and then she told me what she was... and what I would become. I'll never forget her words: 'Maybe I will be yours, maybe no. If I am not then at least you will live forever, just like me, and when you find your female, I do not mind to share.' I retched after that." His lips curled into a dark smile. "But as you can see, her blood stayed in my system despite my reaction."

"Sounds like the wine has done all the damage it can. I get why you hate it." He'd been forced into this—tricked by a female driven by lust. As his words settled in my mind, I realized what she had done to him was no better than what the king had done to me.

"What about you? What's something you hate—besides males?" he asked, taking a bite of Alfredo.

166

"Everything."

He snorted. "Bullshit. You don't hate your sisters. And you definitely don't hate annihilating your opponents in battle."

"I enjoy not being weak," I countered, taking a bite of my dinner to hide the smirk threatening to surface. He wasn't wrong. I didn't hate being powerful. So why was I fighting the urge to smile?

"Fair enough. I'll give you a different question—one you don't have to answer right now. Tell me something you love, something that actually makes you happy."

"My sisters," I answered instantly.

"Yes, but be more specific. What do you love about them? What do you love doing with them?" His question cut deeper, stripping away the surface.

I hesitated. "I love watching them. The way they smile and talk—to each other, to others."

What I didn't say was that I envied it. My conversations with my sisters were always brief, focused on battle and survival. But when they spoke to each other, it was effortless. They were softer, gentler, more capable of joy than I had ever been.

"When we get your missing sister back, tell her that. Tell them both."

Silence settled between us as we ate; the only sound was the quiet clink of utensils and the occasional tap-tap of his laptop keys. I drank straight from the bottle, letting the bitter warmth of the wine settle low in my chest. When both tins were empty, I carried the trash to the kitchen along with our forks.

167

Returning to the living room, I cleared my throat. "You were right. If I slit my throat, I'm useless. So I need you to bite me."

His throat bobbed, his eyes locking onto mine. "Just tap my arm when you want me to stop."

I nodded and sat at the other end of the couch, let my head fall back, and closed my eyes, willing the tension to drain from my body.

I heard him rise and felt the subtle shift of air as he moved behind me. His hands settled on either side of my head, steady but not restraining. I braced for his touch—just his mouth, just his teeth. His hands wouldn't grip me, wouldn't pin me down. His teeth wouldn't be bruising or cruel.

No. Fin was only doing what I had asked him to do. Nothing more.

He wasn't one of those gladiators I had been forced to fight.

He wasn't the king who had delighted in my suffering.

"I'm going to bite you now, so don't hit me." His voice was close, his breath warm against my throat. Then his teeth sank in. A sharp pinch, then the familiar pop as they pierced deep. Pain flared—brief, fleeting—before pleasure overtook it, a wave of relief washing through me as the burning itch in my vocal cords finally eased. His lips sealed over the wound, his mouth pulling, drawing my blood in slow, rhythmic swallows. Each pull sent tingling heat through my body, the relief almost intoxicating. I let out a breath, my hand instinctively rising to the back of his head, fingers threading into his thick hair. He jerked slightly at the touch but didn't pull away.

168

If anything, his drinking slowed, each swallow growing lazier, more indulgent. His scent filled my senses—frankincense and myrrh, rich and heady. His hair was soft between my fingers, his mouth warm and slick against my throat. His breath tickled my skin, slow and deep. *When was the last time someone had breathed that close to me? When was the last time my fingers had laced into a female's hair? Had they ever laced into a male's?*

The seal of his lips broke. His tongue swept over the puncture wounds, lapping up the last trickle of blood before it could run. He didn't move away, and neither did I. We stayed there, suspended in something unspoken, hearts beating in the quiet. Gently, slowly, I pulled my fingers from his hair, my hand feeling empty without his head cupped in my palm. *Was I shaking?* I didn't shoot up from where I sat, an exercise in trust. Trust was something I never thought I'd have for anyone other than my sisters after Helen.

"If I take more, you might lose consciousness right here." My neck didn't feel his breath, telling me he'd straightened behind me, but I hadn't felt his hands leave the back of the sofa. "That would leave you vulnerable—too vulnerable to sleep here."

I opened my eyes to find him looking down at me, a slight heat to his face, a darkening in his eyes. Blood. He was a Vampire who'd just fed. Gently, I sat up, feeling light-headed. He was right; had he taken much more, I'd have been unconscious. I was on the verge of it now. I felt light, almost drunk in a way. I got to my feet and walked to my bedroom, shutting the door behind me and locking it. Not that a lock would do any good against immortals, but I needed it. I felt vulnerable. Looking at the bed, I did something I hadn't done in a very long time: I pulled back the

169

blankets, settled into the soft mattress, closed my eyes, and let myself drift into sleep, the feel of Fin's lips on my throat still tingling through my senses.

Fin...

I moved behind the couch, positioning myself directly behind her. My heart pounded a steady drumbeat in my chest at her nearness. Did she have any idea what it did to me, being this close yet unable to touch her? As a Vampire, I craved her blood. As a bonded male, I craved her—her flesh, her scent, her voice, her very existence. She craved only release from the curse of her vocal cords, her price for immortality.

Bracing my hands against the back of the couch, I leaned in, angling my head to sink my fangs into her vocal cords. Her throat, delicate and exposed, was mere inches from my lips. I swallowed hard—gods help me, I was nervous. For both our sakes, I told her I was going to bite her now. My teeth pierced her flesh, slicing through skin and tendon before finally breaking through her vocal cords. I forced my grip on the couch to loosen, my immortal strength threatening to splinter the frame.

I pulled, drawing her coppery, bourbon-laced blood into my mouth, savoring the warmth as it spread over my tongue and the feel of her soft skin against my lips. My heart pounded in my ears, the world shrinking down to the roaring rush of her blood, the sound overwhelming. I'd been hard since the moment she asked me to bite her, wanting more—so much more—than just my teeth inside her flesh. Her fingers grazed my ear, threading into my hair. I jolted, my newly beating heart stuttering in shock.

170

Her fingers splayed over my scalp, kneading in rhythm with each pull of my mouth against her throat. I slowed, savoring the sensation of her touching me. Hibiscus and sea salt filled my senses, her scent wrapping around me. The gentle swell of her breasts lingered just within my periphery—a temptation I ached to look at.

Her scent surrounded me, the warmth of her throat against my lips, her deceptively delicate hand tangled in my hair—I felt myself slipping, losing control. I knew every inch of her body; the memory of her stripping that first night burned into my mind, an image I could never forget. My breath hitched as the image twisted—her blood-covered torso in the bathtub, her throat gaping from the deep gash she had carved into herself. I ran my tongue over the small wound I had left on her throat, forcing myself to break the seal of my lips against her skin. Silence stretched between us as I savored the lingering touch of her fingers in my hair. When she finally pulled away, an ache settled deep in my chest.

I straightened, forcing space between us when all I wanted was to close it—to touch her, taste her, and trace the curve of her throat with my lips and teeth. "If I take more, you might lose consciousness right here." Removing my hands from the sofa, I put even more distance between us in an effort to control my own urges. "That would leave you vulnerable—too vulnerable to sleep here." If only she would allow herself to be vulnerable enough for more than just my bite. If only she would let me kiss every scar, let me atone for not being there when she had been brutalized. To erase the cruelty she'd endured with nothing but tenderness and satisfaction. All these thoughts swirled in my head as I gazed at the female who refused to be mine when the bond begged otherwise. The female whose strength and resilience called to me on a level I couldn't explain.

I watched her rise, her steps unsteady as she made her way to the room she had claimed for the day. Every instinct in me begged to help her, but I had learned that first night—she wouldn't allow it. She was fierce, untouchable—strong and fluid like the sea. Despite the bland tone she held most of the time, I knew there was an ocean rolling beneath the surface. She cared deeply for her sisters, but her words indicated that even with them, she felt like an outcast. She had made herself an island—jagged cliffs, crashing waves, a fortress against the world. And Gods help me, I wanted to reach her.

Ella...

When I finally woke, it had taken me a moment to realize where I was, tucked comfortably under the blankets. Comfort wasn't something I was used to. I was used to waking with the feel of dried blood on my body and the familiar slant of the tub against my back. I pushed myself into a sitting position and looked around, thinking how this was what my sisters woke to every morning. Casting off the blankets, I got out of bed and stretched, finding the lack of tightness in my body both refreshing and strange. This was the second time Fin had helped me find this strange kind of rest that was so unfamiliar.

I got out of bed, grabbed my bag, and headed for the door, intending to take a shower, if for no other reason than to make things feel more normal—wake up and wash away the night. I opened the door and found Fin sitting against the wall. "What are you doing?" I demanded, disliking how it reminded me of being a prisoner in Atlantis.

"The sun was coming through the curtains and hitting the couch, so I had to move."

I narrowed my eyes at his response. "But why here?"

"So I could hear your heartbeat." Closing the laptop, he stood and looked down at me. "It's comforting, even if that's not what you want to hear. When I try to sleep, I'm plagued by nightmares of it stopping and never starting again—nightmares of your lifeless body, broken and bloody in that bathtub, where your head has been cut completely off instead of just a slit across your throat." He took a step closer to me, glancing at my bag. "If you're going to slit your throat, let me know now before I go to sleep. I won't leave you unprotected."

I won't leave you unprotected. I couldn't explain what those words did to me. My lips parted as I looked up at him, his dark eyes pained as he gazed at me. He wasn't demanding I not do it, not outright, but his eyes were. "I'm just taking a shower; you can rest."

Chapter 16

Ella...

When the sun was finally low enough, we left the safehouse and began checking the locations that lined up with the name the Priestess had given us. Kassie and Clay had already checked several locations, leaving us with only a handful to go. It took us nearly two hours to reach our first location: Lola's in Tyler, TX. It didn't take long to determine that it was nothing more than a sandwich shop. Two hours later, we reached our second location—and our second dead end. The drive from Anna, TX, was another hour and a half of wasted time as we reached our third dead end. We were six hours into the night with nothing to show for it.

"The next stop is Irving. This one's a restaurant and lounge," Fin said as we got back into the truck.

"If this is another dead end, we're going back to Lufkin so I can kick that Priestess's ass."

"Agreed," Fin said, frustration clear in his tone as he put the truck in drive and pulled out of the parking lot.

"She could have at least narrowed it down to a fucking area. We're wasting our damn time looking for a lead on this

174

name! There are dozens of fucking Lola's in Texas!" Frustration tightened my chest and tensed my muscles.

"At least your sister and her male can search during the day, so we're covering twice as much ground." He glanced at me, then back at the road, guilt lighting his eyes.

"Fuck off with your guilt for being a Vampire. I'm over it; you should be too. Just fucking drive so we can cover some ground." I didn't do well with feelings—guilt or otherwise. I had too much guilt of my own. Had I fought back harder the day we were taken on that ship, my sisters would never have suffered in Atlantis. Most days, I'd made peace with that weakness because I'd been a mortal child, but other days, I hated myself. The days I hated myself the most were the days I resented them for falling asleep while I had to slit my throat just to find a few hours of peace. How I coped wasn't their fault. Their nightmares haunted them just as mine haunted me.

"Sure thing." His response was short and sweet. I wasn't sure if I'd upset him—not that I gave a flying fuck.

After another thirty minutes, we reached the next Lola's on our list. "Hopefully, we can find an immortal who's not going to give us some vague-ass shit to go off of like Nia." I wasn't feeling guilty. Nope. No guilt. He was a male and didn't deserve shit from me.

"I'm surprised you remembered her name," Fin mused as we walked into the establishment, his clipped tone from earlier gone, giving me some relief. Not because I cared, but because I didn't have time to deal with his feelings.

175

"She left an impression." I scanned the place, noting the mix of humans and immortals. I didn't care about him. I needed to find my sister—that's why I was getting emotional.

"Let's check out the bartender and see what he can tell us," Fin said, making his way toward the counter, a wall of liquor glinting in amber tones behind it.

When we reached the counter, the bartender's nostrils flared as he took us in, no doubt identifying us by our scents. The mix of whiskey and leather filled my nose as he neared us, telling me he was a Goblin. To immortals with less heightened senses, like Witches and myself, they smelled more like an engine. "Your hibiscus perfume is interesting, Miss."

"Does someone named Lola work here?" Fin interrupted before I could answer.

The Goblin's eyes flashed, and he gave a curt nod. "She's in the back taking inventory. Just a sec." He walked to the door labeled *STAFF ONLY*, set just to the side of the counter. Moments later, he returned and glanced between the two of us. "She said to send you back. She gets touchy when she's doing inventory and someone interrupts her. Just a heads up."

"Thanks," Fin said, and we walked through the door to find a thick, curvy Latina holding a clipboard. She smelled of black currant and jasmine, telling me she was an Elf, even if she didn't look the part.

"Let me guess, Nia sent you? Yeah, the bitch texted me that you were coming. I swear, I don't even know her or how she got my damn number," Lola complained, taking inventory without looking up from her clipboard.

176

"Can you help us or not?" I grated, already sick of this. She might not look like an Elf, but her high-and-mighty attitude was fucking spot on.

"I don't know, maybe. What are you looking for again?"

"Where to get the things on this list," Fin said, handing her the paper.

She looked it over and let out a whistle. "Dangerous ingredients, if you ask me. I think there might be a place in Kansas to get Gorgon scales where you won't die."

"Where in Kansas?" I demanded, fed up with the bullshit leads.

"Look, I'm not a freaking GPS. I just remember someone mentioning getting them there once. That's the best I've got. I'm an Elf trying to make a living, not a Witch buying shit off the black market." She turned and looked at me. "You want to find Gorgon scales? Find black market locations in Kansas. That's all I can offer. Now, if you don't mind, I'm trying to work."

"Thanks for your time," Fin said. He glanced at me and nodded toward the door. "Let's get going. We're running out of dark and have a lot of ground to cover."

"Where the fuck are we going? You can't seriously be suggesting we blindly drive to Kansas?" Anger sharpened my voice as I followed him out.

"I'll reach out to my contacts and see what locations they come up with as we head that way. We don't need an exact location, just an idea of where to search. The goal is to find your sister. I can hack cameras faster than we can search locations."

177

"Then what the fuck have we been doing all damn night?" I demanded, heading for the exit, drawing curious looks from the patrons.

"Why don't we talk about this in the truck?" he suggested, his eyes scanning our surroundings.

"Whatever." I shoved past him and headed for the truck, watching the lights blink as he unlocked it behind me.

"Do you know how many places there are to get the shit on this list?" Fin demanded as he climbed into the truck. "We needed this lead to narrow it down to one state instead of ten. In those ten states my contacts gave me, there are multiple locations to search, and not all of them have cameras for me to hack."

"I get it. Just drive." I turned to stare out the window. Inside me, a storm raged—fear, stress, and anger swirling, tightening my body with tension, while the itch clawed at my throat, stretching its tendrils down to the pit of my stomach, demanding to be fed.

"You should tell your other sister where we're headed. They might find another lead. I have a safehouse near Duncan, Oklahoma, where we should make it before sunrise."

"So you're telling me we won't even make it to fucking Kansas? Damn it." I slammed my head back against the headrest. Sighing, I closed my eyes. "I have to remind myself that they're searching for these things too. They have to travel as well. I'm just hoping we can catch up with them." Hopelessness gnawed at me, threatening to take control of the storm, but I'd been down that path before.

178

"Also, the Lycan is traveling with an unwilling companion. If your sister's anything like you, she's not making it easy for him."

A smile tugged at my lips as I thought about the hell Theia was undoubtedly putting the Lycan through. "Kassie's the sweet one; Theia's violent and rebellious. I hope she's left some marks on him."

***

Ella...

We spent three days tracking leads before finally being directed toward Nebraska, eager to leave Kansas and its dead ends behind. Fin would bite me each night, offering a fleeting release from the itch. I'd drift into sleep, nestled beneath the blankets, a sensation I was quickly coming to appreciate after years of finding solace at the edge of a blade and waking in dried blood. Each night ended with Fin's lips on my throat, his teeth buried deep in my vocal cords, and his breath warm against my skin. Lacing my fingers through his hair and gripping the back of his head had become second nature. But the itch remained, still demanding satisfaction.

Our next lead brought us to an enchanted immortal bar near the Kansas-Nebraska border, cloaked to mortals by powerful spells. We entered the bar, seeking new leads and information. I also needed a drink to take the edge off—both from the never-ending search for Theia and being around the Vampire. I couldn't shake the tension since Fin told me I was his blooded female. Never in my existence had I imagined I'd be a Vampire's fated female. Fin was the only male who had touched me and

179

walked away unscathed since the fall of Atlantis. The truth was, I needed him. Not just to help me find Theia but to satisfy my itch with his teeth and the brush of his lips on my throat. I...needed to touch him while he did that.

"Finlay, mon amour," a stunning female called out, her thick French accent curling around each word as we approached the bar.

"Colette," Fin muttered, his eyes closing in annoyance before he turned to face her.

"I thought it was you! Tell me you've found your female, and she just doesn't compare to me," the French bitch purred, placing her hands on his chest and pressing herself against him.

Fin grasped her wrists and gently pushed her away. "It's been five hundred years; let it go already."

Colette pouted, arching her back and pressing her barely covered breasts upward. "Mon amour, don't be that way. We had such fun together, no?"

"You got me killed. Find someone else to toy with," Fin said, casting a glance at me.

"She's got nice tits. I'd hit it," I said, waving the bartender over. Until now, I'd just been observing the exchange, but Fin's glance had signaled me to join in.

"Looks like someone is interested in my charms," Colette said as I felt her fingers trail down my arm. I glanced at her with indifference, carefully noting how her touch felt on every level, before she questioned, "Are you the reason I hear his heart beating?"

"What can I get you?" the bartender asked.

180

"Shot of Crown and an ink pen for the lady," I said calmly. He pulled the pen from his pocket, setting it on the counter, then turned to grab the Crown from the back shelf.

"Are you giving me your number then?" Colette purred in her thick accent, edging closer, her eyelids lowering seductively.

I grabbed the pen and turned to face her. "Let me start with your first question. Yes, I'm the reason his heart is beating." A slight smile tugged at the corner of my lips as the bartender set my drink down. I tossed back the shot, adjusted my grip on the pen, slammed the glass on the counter, and spun around to face Colette. "The pen is for following through with what I said about hitting you."

Without hesitation, I stabbed the pen into her eye, sending her reeling backward, screaming in agony as blood poured down her face. I acted on the jealousy burning at the thought of her touching Fin. The Vampire was *mine*.

"Bloody hell," Fin gasped in astonishment as I advanced on the blood-sucking whore.

"Get up and fight, you worthless cunt," I snarled, taking a step closer.

"No one messes with my female!" a male voice shouted, charging toward me.

Before I could react, Fin's hand vanished into the larger male's chest, reappearing with the heart in his grasp. "I could say the same—but she hasn't decided I'm worthy yet." Fin dropped the heart and glanced around the now-silent bar. A group of well-built males started walking toward us. "Ella, I think we've started something messy here."

181

A chuckle escaped my lips as I walked toward the advancing group of immortals and inhaled deeply. "Smells like cat litter in here," I taunted, recognizing the coconut and lime scent of Leopard Shifters.

"You're going to pay for that—and for her," one of them growled, nodding toward a silently sobbing Colette.

"Ella, maybe you should—I don't know—hum a tune or something," Fin said nervously, trying to move in front of me.

These males weren't like the Merfolk we'd faced—they were Shifters. Shifters were inherently stronger than other immortals. I wasn't like other immortals, though—I was the daughter of the God of War. The thrill of this fight sent a spark of excitement through me that only my sisters would understand. We were born for battle.

"Where's the fun in that?" I asked before launching myself at the Shifter who'd spoken to me. I leaped at him, locking my legs around his neck and using my momentum to twist and slam him to the ground.

Catching movement out of the corner of my eye, I clenched my fists and drove my left elbow into the gut of my approaching attacker, knocking the wind out of him and forcing him back a few steps. Another Shifter knocked me back with a blow, but I threw my hands over my head, flipping onto my feet and executing a swift high kick that connected with the jaw of the same male I'd elbowed, sending him sprawling.

I plunged my hand into his chest and ripped his heart from his body, looking up to see Fin using his fangs to rip the throat out of the male who'd knocked me backward. The male I'd thrown to the ground with my legs scrambled to his feet and charged at Fin.

182

Without hesitation, I ducked and charged at him, my shoulder slamming into his abdomen from the side. My arms wrapped around him as I drove him to the floor.

Pushing upward, I lashed out with my fingers curled like talons, tearing out his throat. Blood sprayed across my face and chest.

A shriek of horror pulled my attention away from where I sat, panting on top of the male I'd just rendered unconscious. Colette was staring at the four panther Shifters Fin, and I had taken on. "You killed them!"

I looked around, taking in the males' prone bodies. "Only for a few hours." I tilted my head and smiled at her. "Touch my Vampire again, and I'll finish the job—starting with you. But you? Oh, I'll enjoy killing you, Colette." She scrambled to her feet and bolted for the door without a glance back. "Shame. I really did enjoy hitting that."

"Damn it! Now I have to clean this up. Just leave before you make an even bigger mess. Damn violent types, ruining my night," the bartender muttered as he grabbed a mop bucket from behind the bar.

"Make them do it when they wake up," I said, shoving to my feet and ignoring the handful of other patrons gawking at us.

"Get out!" he bellowed, throwing a finger toward the door.

"We're leaving," Fin said, motioning for me to follow him out the back door to the dark parking lot, his eyes scanning me with concern.

We climbed into the truck in silence and pulled out of the parking lot. I didn't have to ask where we were going. I flexed my

183

fingers, the sticky blood still warm on them and up my arm. I glanced at Fin, seeing blood splattered across his face, shirt, and arms. Had I just told that slut he was mine? Yes, I had. I studied his profile, his eyes briefly glancing at me before returning to the road. What the hell was I feeling?

"There's another immortal bar that should be tied to the black market. After we clean up at the safehouse, I'll check how far it is, and we'll head that way." His voice broke the silence. We'd spent most of the night hunting for leads already. "Do you..." he began, clearing his throat, then glanced at me again. "Do I need to bite you after that fight? I know you asked me last time."

"Yes." My response was nearly choked, and I turned my gaze away from him. He wasn't like the males who had abused me—neither in build nor personality. He didn't stir fear in me—not in the way other males did.

I realized he stirred something terrifying inside me: *desire*. My mind replayed the scene from the bar when he'd ripped out the throat of the male who'd struck me. The way he'd looked at me—his eyes searching my face and body, not hungrily, but filled with concern as we'd walked out of the bar. He'd said I wasn't his until I accepted him, just moments before that. Was he waiting on me?

Twenty minutes later, we walked into the safehouse, and I dropped my bags to the right of the door, not even bothering to look for a room. As soon as Fin shut the door, my hand fisted in his shirt, and I shoved him back against it. My lips locked onto his, and he went stiff for a moment before one of his hands cupped either side of my face, returning the kiss. I pulled away,

184

breathing heavily, my eyes feeling wide. My heart pounded in my ears.

"Are you okay?" Concern filled his eyes as he gazed at my face.

"I need a shower." My fucking heart felt like it was going to explode out of my chest. There was so much inside me. Quickly putting distance between us, I grabbed my bag and walked to the bathroom, the one joined to the bedroom I'd spotted when we'd entered. I was relieved he seemed to own safehouses that were built the same.

I shut the bathroom door and stripped off my blood-soaked clothes. My eyes flicked to the door, wondering if he would come in after I'd kissed him. Turning on the shower, I stepped in and began washing the blood from my body and hair.

Standing under the hot spray as the last of the soap washed off, I thought about what I was feeling—the roaring itch in my throat. I opened my eyes, turned off the water, stepped out, and dried off.

Chapter 17

Ella...

"Damn it," I muttered, wrapping the towel around my body. I walked out of the bathroom, out of the bedroom, and across the hall. Fin's door was closed, but I walked in without knocking, not wanting to lose my nerve. Just as I entered, Fin stepped out of his bathroom, a towel clutched around his waist. My eyes scanned his body; he was lean, but muscles were etched across his torso, with a V-shaped cut disappearing into the towel around his hips.

He froze, his eyes locking onto mine as I dragged my gaze back up his body to meet his.

"I need you," I said, my voice barely a whisper.

"Ella, I need you to be crystal clear about what you want here. You're standing in my room wearing nothing but a towel, and I—" He swallowed hard, "I want you in ways you might not want me."

"Ditch the towel and get on the bed. How's that for clear?"

I dropped my towel, letting it fall to the floor. No turning back now.

186

"Shit." Fin let out a breath as he walked to the bed, his eyes locked on mine the entire time. He dropped the towel and sat down. My gaze raked over his muscular build as I moved toward him. His chest was sculpted, leading into the outline of his abs. My eyes fell to the thing between his legs. Had I ever truly looked at one before? After all those years spent battered and raped, I didn't think I had ever truly looked at a man's cock.

"Ella, we don't have to—"

"Shut up." I cut him off and closed the distance between us in a few quick strides. He looked up at me as I stood in front of him. "I've never wanted a male's touch before. Do you understand that? The only feelings a male has ever given me are pain and anger."

"I'll end anyone who touches you." His eyes locked with mine, even as I stood naked in front of him.

"The feeling is mutual. I still want to end that cunt for touching you. You are mine, Leech." The corner of my mouth twitched up as I called him that name. I was so nervous I had to find some way to calm myself down. I wasn't used to feeling nervous like this.

"Anything you want, Songbird," he replied. I put my hands on his shoulders and straddled his lap, his warmth seeping into my skin, his erection bobbing between us in the space I'd left. His hands reached out and settled on my hips, making me jerk. "I'll never hurt you, Ella." One of his hands slid up my side and around to my back. "Let me show you how a female is supposed to be treated—how a female is supposed to be worshiped, kissed, and touched."

187

He'd been showing me the entire time we'd been together—giving me patience, respect, and trust.

"Show me," I whispered, my voice trembling. He leaned forward, his lips brushing over my collarbone. My head tipped back at the warmth of his touch. My heart pounded almost painfully in my chest, but his touch was something I didn't want to stop, even if part of me was still afraid. He pulled me closer to his lap, his erection pressing between my thighs. Fear licked up my spine, but I pushed it down. He wouldn't hurt me.

"I'll go as slow as you need me to," he murmured against my skin, lightly nipping at my throat. "I'll stop if you tell me to. You're in control here."

"I don't know how this works—with a male." Not willingly, anyway. I didn't need to tell him that, though.

He gave a soft laugh against my throat. "Then should I start like I'm a female? Because the thought of tasting you, of worshiping you..." His tongue ran the length of my throat before his teeth tugged at my ear. "The thought of tasting more than your blood has crossed my mind."

I turned my head to look at him, only for his lips to meet mine. His hand slipped up between my shoulders as the kiss deepened. His tongue flicked against my lips, and mine darted out in response. My nipples brushed against his chest as my back arched, and I re-adjusted my position on his lap, trying to get closer without even realizing it.

I was growing wet, but I was still nervous. Breaking the kiss, I looked up at his face. I'd dreamed of his face between my legs once. And I wasn't afraid of him. I wasn't afraid of what he'd do to me.

188

"I want you to bite me—" my teeth raked over my bottom lip, "—between my legs."

"Your wish is my command," he said, quickly flipping me onto my back on the mattress. My breath hitched as fear battled with desire at the way he maneuvered me. "Tell me when to stop."

Gods, the way he reassured me.

His eyes were dark as he looked down at me, then slowly kissed my stomach, his hands lightly brushing over my skin. I spread my legs a little wider for him as one of his arms slipped behind my thigh, then the other. His hands gripped my ass, lifting me slightly. I was spread wide for him for just a heartbeat before his tongue slid up my pussy.

My hips jerked at the sensation like electricity shooting through my body. My core throbbed, and I gasped just as his lips locked onto my clit and he began to suck. His tongue, lips, and teeth teased and nipped at my core, driving me mad until I finally felt his fangs pierce me.

A sound like a whimper escaped me as my head fell back in pleasure, my hands fisting in the sheets. The feel of him sucking my blood, his fangs buried in me, and his hands gripping the cheeks of my ass sent wave after wave of ecstasy through me. My body shuddered with release, my heart pounding in my ears. His teeth slipped out of me, and his tongue lapped at me hungrily, drinking in the mix of my orgasm and my blood.

"That's it, Songbird, cum for me. You taste so fucking good." His breath was hot on my thighs as he kissed and nipped at them, making me twitch from the tickling sensation. He let out a low chuckle. "If you'll let me, I'll make your body do that many,

189

many more times." He looked up at me, his dark eyes dancing with a wicked light that made my heart skip a beat. *Many more times?*

"If you take too much blood, I'll just pass out." Not that it would be a bad way to pass out.

A half-smile curved his full lips. "I don't have to bite you to give you that kind of pleasure."

His arm slipped from under me to over my thigh, bending at the elbow, his hand resting in front of his face, still between my legs and on top of my core. "Like this, for instance." His thumb flicked over my clit. "While I do this." His tongue licked up my center, his flat teeth raking against my sensitive flesh, his thumb rubbing circles while his hand kneaded my ass cheek. My hands fisted in the sheets again as my body arched off the bed, and a moan slipped from my lips.

"V-Vampire," I gasped as he pinched and rolled my clit between his fingers, his mouth still doing devilish things between my thighs. "I'm cumming." His growl rumbled through me, his hot breath coming in huffs as he greedily drank down my second release. When it finally ended, I lay there panting, my hand clenching and unclenching in the sheets. My legs fell weakly to either side of him.

"I'm not done worshiping you just yet, Songbird. But we can take a break if you need to recover. I've got two weeks of daydreams to make up for."

I pushed myself up on my elbows and arched a brow. "Are you trying to kill me?" Males had tried before, but never like this. Like this, I might be willing to die.

190

He arched a brow. "Are you saying you want me to stop? Two little orgasms are all you wanted? Surely I can do better than that for you."

I swallowed, knowing what he was asking. Could I do it? Could I take a male's cock willingly into my body? I wondered as I looked down at him.

If you'll let me, your wish is my command. I won't leave you unprotected. This male—he wasn't pushing me for anything, not in the state we were in. He'd given me pleasure twice now without seeking any for himself.

"Let's see what you've got then, Leech," I added with a small smile. I was going to do it. I was going to have sex with a male on my terms.

He smiled and pushed himself up onto his forearms, kissing his way up my abdomen. "I'm going to make sure you enjoy every moment of this. I want it burned into your memory so deep that it replaces every bad thing that's ever cast a shadow over you." His words came in hot breaths against my sensitive flesh. "If I could erase every scar from your body, I would." He kissed the jagged line across my abdomen. "If I could turn back time and eviscerate those who wronged you, I'd do it again and again until the world ran red with their blood."

His right hand ran up my body, up my throat, and cupped my chin. "I'm your goddamn slave, Ella. If you don't like how someone looks at you, I'll end them. Guilt be damned."

Before I could respond, his lips were on mine, his hand moving to the back of my leg, gently guiding it up so that my knee was bent. I followed suit with the other leg. I could feel the head of his erection brushing against my slick folds. I braced

191

myself for the pain that would come as he entered me—the ripping and bleeding I knew all too well.

He pressed forward, but no pain came. My body stretched around him—pressure and slight discomfort as he slowly slid in, then pulled back a fraction and pushed forward further. The discomfort faded with the second thrust of his hips, pushing himself deeper inside, but still not completely. He leaned forward, his lips grazing my neck as he pulled back again. "Open your eyes. I want to look at you when I'm fully seated inside. I need to know I'm not hurting you."

My eyes flashed open, my lips parting as I looked at him. Even now, he was worried for my comfort when he had what all males wanted right beneath him.

"Ready for me, Songbird?" In response, I rolled my hips, seating him completely inside me. His eyes fluttered, and a groan escaped his lips, mingling with my own.

"Gods, Ella. I've waited an eternity to feel you." His hips pulled back, and he pushed forward again. My back arched, my hands gripping his arms. "I'm going to make my little Songbird sing," he said, his forehead pressing against mine as his hips began to move faster. His heavy balls bounced against me with each thrust. My pleasure was a tight band, growing tighter with each thrust of his hips. My nails dug into his skin as I tried to pull him closer, even though he was already as close as he could get. I couldn't get enough of him. The smell of frankincense and myrrh filled my nostrils.

Just when I thought it couldn't feel any better, he slipped a hand between us, his fingers toying with my clit. I moaned as pleasure rolled through my body, my back arching into his

192

movements, my legs wrapping around him. Then, as I felt myself nearing that peak again, his fangs sank into the side of my throat, and I exploded. A cry of pleasure tore through me as he snarled against my flesh. His hips pumped fiercely into me before he reached a shuddering climax of his own.

His hand ripped from between us, slamming into the mattress beside my head. His breathing came in heavy pants against my throat as he held his shuddering body above mine. Slowly, he pulled his fangs from my neck and gently kissed the bite, his lips trailing over my skin, placing soft kisses along my jaw. He eased himself to the side, no longer holding me against the mattress.

I pushed up on my elbow and looked at him, my chest rising and falling in tandem with my heavy breathing. He opened his eyes and met my gaze, a soft smile on his lips. I realized I was smiling, too.

"You lied." His smile faded, replaced by a look of confusion.

"You said *many* more times, and yet here you are, completely exhausted. Pathetic." I could feel the challenge flashing in my eyes as I smiled down at him.

His smile returned. "You'll have to excuse me while I catch my breath; after all, I am over five hundred years old."

I snorted. "I'm over twelve thousand. Try again, Leech."

He started laughing. "Fine, you're older, but I haven't had a heartbeat in five hundred years, and you just made mine feel like it was exploding."

"Pussy."

193

He pushed up onto his elbow and looked at me then. "What did you just call me?"

"I called you a pussy. Should I have called you a weak-ass bitch?"

His lips parted, and he rolled his jaw slightly as he took in my face. The next thing I knew, he was pulling me on top of him, dragging my face to his so he could kiss me.

"It's your turn to work for it, Songbird." His hand laced into my hair as he leaned up, his cheek brushing against mine, his tongue licking up the side of my face. "I want to watch you come apart as you ride me, finding your pleasure again and again." I could feel him growing hard beneath me as his words brushed against my ear. "I want to watch you take control of me. I want you to tell me how and where to touch you."

My lips parted at his words. He wanted me to take control of him? I pushed myself up and looked at him, meeting his hungry gaze. Moving my body, I adjusted until he was at my entrance, then slowly slid down until our bodies were fully joined, never breaking eye contact. He shuddered as I lifted myself and lowered again. So. Very. Slowly. "I want you to use your fingers again, like you did before, while I ride you. I want your mouth on my breasts, my nipples between your teeth."

Gods, did he do what I said! He pulled me down with one hand, and his mouth sucked my breast in, where my nipple was nipped and sucked and flicked with his tongue. His other hand was between us, his fingers tormenting my clit as I rode him. My nails rasped over his shoulders, and sounds I didn't know I was capable of escaped my body as I drove myself to another orgasm with his help.

194

Chapter 18

Ella...

I woke under the blankets, my body draped haphazardly over Fin's. His scent filled my nostrils, and images of yesterday flooded my mind. I didn't move, only opening my eyes after a moment. His heartbeat thrummed steadily beneath my ear, his arms draped loosely around me. Panic threatened to take hold as I lay there, tangled in his embrace.

"How did you sleep, Songbird?" His voice made me jump, but his hands moved gently, rubbing my arm and back. "I didn't mean to startle you. I just noticed your breathing change and thought you were awake," he murmured.

"I thought you were still asleep," I admitted, hesitant to move despite his gentle touch. Touch wasn't something I was used to—but it was something I craved. *This* kind of touch.

"I've been awake for a while. I just didn't want to disturb you." His gaze softened. "I've never seen you look so peaceful." I pushed myself up at his words, and he released me, shifting to sit against the headboard. "I'm going to take a shower. Care to join me?"

195

"I'll use my own," I said flatly, scooting to the edge of the bed. I'd looked peaceful. He hadn't wanted to disturb me. Had anyone ever been that… considerate?

"Ella, did I do something wrong?"

I sat at the edge of the bed, my gaze fixed on the floor. "No, I just need to think." He'd given me so many words, so many confessions. The least I could do was offer him this much honesty.

"Okay. Just know I'm here if thinking turns into needing to talk. I know you don't talk much, but… I'm here."

I rolled my eyes and stood. "You're such a girl," I muttered, striding out and crossing the hall to my room. I grabbed my bag, hesitated—then turned back, the emptiness of my own room suddenly unbearable. "Not a word," I warned, striding into his bathroom, and leaving the door wide open as I turned on the shower. "Vampire, are you coming?" I called as I stepped under the spray, not bothering to look back.

It didn't take long for Fin to join me. He slipped in behind me, stepping under the stream. "I'll wash your back if you wash mine," he murmured. He was careful—not touching me, even in the close space. Even after everything we'd done last night, he still respected my space. And damn, if that wasn't hot.

"I'll only wash your back if you scratch my itch, Leech."

His tongue, lips, and teeth teased and nipped at my neck from behind, his hands resting lightly on my arms. "I think I'm starting to like your insults, Songbird." My pulse kicked up as his body brushed against mine from behind. "You're in complete control, Ella. You call all the shots with me." His lips brushed over my shoulder. The last time he'd been behind me, we were

196

fighting that Warlock on our first night together. My heart had raced for an entirely different reason then.

"Shut up and bite me already," I whispered, tilting my head to the side and exposing my throat. Was I still nervous? Yes. But I wasn't weak enough to let that trauma control me any longer. It had dominated my existence for the last twelve thousand years, and I was done allowing that. His teeth sank into my flesh, and I felt him pull me flush against him, claiming me completely.

One hand found my breast while the other drifted lower, fingers teasing between my thighs. He wasn't sucking my blood, just holding me in place with his teeth, and I fucking loved it. His erection pressed against my backside as his fingers pinched and stroked, his tongue tracing slow, torturous circles around his buried fangs. He withdrew his fangs and turned me to face him; his lips stained crimson as he kissed me—hungry, possessive. Pressing me against the shower wall, he lifted me effortlessly, thrusting deep into my aching core.

My nails raked across his back as he drove himself between my legs. I moaned into his mouth before dragging my lips from his and sinking my blunt teeth into his shoulder. Fin groaned, his grip bruising as he drove deeper, faster until he shattered—his release triggering mine in a rush of heat and pleasure. "Fuck, Ella... yes."

"What. The. Fuck?" Kassie's voice sliced through the steam and the aftermath of our pleasure.

"Shit," Fin cursed, nearly losing his grip on me as he turned to face my sister and Clay—both frozen in the doorway.

197

Kassie's expression twisted in sheer shock before she spun on her heel, nearly plowing into her mate.

"Sorry," Clay muttered, shutting the door behind them without daring to look.

Fin chuckled. "Not what I expected. I thought she'd try to kick my ass—like you would."

"That explains why you almost dropped me. Now put me down so we can finish washing," I said flatly.

"Sorry about that. In my defense, it's slippery in here."

"Fuck off." I turned my back to him, having officially hit my talking quota for the moment.

***

Ella...

I made my way out of the bedroom while Fin dressed, to find Kassie and Clay in the living room, where she was pacing.

"Fucking knock next time," I said as I glared at her.

She stopped and looked at me with huge eyes. "You—you were fucking a male!"

I folded my arms. "His head was between my legs last night. What's your point?"

Clay got up from the couch and disappeared into the kitchen. Good. "You—but he's a *male!*" Her gaze locked on my neck. "Holy shit, you're *bleeding!* He *bit* you?"

"In the neck, the thigh, the shoulder, and between my legs," I informed her, feeling my body get hot all over again. Was this because I'd denied my Siren's Call for so long? Or was it Fin in particular?

"You *told* me to bite you, so I did," Fin said, stepping into the room—his cheeks tinged pink. Was he *blushing?*

198

"And you'll do it again later." I shot him a look before turning toward the window. "Right now, we need to find Theia... once the sun's low enough."

"You're a *freak*." Kassie gawked at me, every inch of her radiating pure disbelief.

"Why are you two always at each other's throats?" Fin asked, stepping up beside me. His hand lifted toward my neck. I flinched. My wet hair slapped against my skin as he hesitated and slowly lowered his hand. "I didn't realize I bit you that hard. Are you all right?"

I glanced at the spot between his neck and shoulder, wondering if I'd left a mark. His shirt hid any evidence. "I'm fine. Just wasn't expecting you to touch me."

He smirked. "You *did* say you'd rip my arm off if I tried."

I shrugged. "Things change." Kassie still gawked at me like I'd grown a second head. I ignored it. "Did you find any leads?"

"No." She kept staring between me and Fin, like her brain was struggling to reboot.

"Then why the fuck did you come into the bathroom without knocking?" I demanded, scanning my golden-haired sister for any signs of healing injuries or distress. If Clay had let her get harmed, there would be hell to pay.

"I heard... well, I *thought* you were in trouble," she admitted, her face flaming red.

Fin raised an eyebrow. "Last night, she put an ink pen through a Vampire's eye, and then the two of us neutralized four Panther Shifters. While your concern for her safety is touching, I

199

believe you should be more concerned for mine should she get mad at me."

"When have I ever needed saving? Leech, do your computer thing, would you? If we can't be intimate, we should be productive in searching for Theia." I effectively dismissed him, averting my full attention back to Kassie.

"At least the nickname I call you is nice," he muttered as he walked to the coffee table, still flushed.

"How—how *long* have you been having sex with males?" Kassie took a cautious step back like Fin carried a damn plague.

"Since we got back from the bar last night. Why?" My voice was flat, unreadable.

Kassie could be as confused as she wanted—if *she* could have a male, then so could I.

Wait. Had I really just thought that?

"You *hate* males! Theia and I have been waiting for you to finally snap and wipe them off the face of the earth—since *Atlantis!*" Kassie threw her arms up before planting one hand on her hip and the other against her forehead.

"That seems a little extreme. She cares about you too much to do that, especially when you obviously like at least one male," Fin chimed in.

"*You* stay out of this!" she snapped, jabbing a finger at him. "You've *corrupted* my sister! I don't even know if it's safe to leave her alone with you anymore."

Fin snorted. "Right. *I'm* the dangerous one. Not the female who threatens me, broke my nose, and tears me down at every turn." He grabbed his laptop and headed for the kitchen but

200

paused at the doorway. "Clay, close the curtains—I'm hiding with you."

"Pussies," I muttered, rolling my eyes—though I couldn't quite stop the smirk tugging at my lips.

"What the hell is going on, Ella?" Kassie's blue eyes pleaded with me—Kassie, who was always understanding, always sweet. Kassie, who had nearly died because of me just weeks ago.

I glanced from her to Fin's retreating back before switching to that long-lost language only we understood.

"He's been biting me since that first night—through the vocal cords. It stops the itch, at least for a while. And I feel... pleasure." I hesitated, then forced myself to continue. *"Last night, I realized he doesn't make me feel like any other male ever has. So I tried something."*

"You tried something?" Her voice shot up an octave. *"That's your explanation?"*

"I slept without needing to lose consciousness for the first time since Helen. Even with her, it wasn't this easy. I can't explain it," I said, my tone growing frustrated. I was doing more talking than I was used to and seemed to be getting nowhere.

"Are you sure this is your choice? Not some hidden Leech power we didn't know about?" Kassie's voice was tight with concern, her pleading eyes searching mine.

"Look into it then. I've never heard of it, and we have been alive longer than most. He didn't force me. He's only touched me twice, and both times, it was to get me out of danger. I'm still thinking about things." I looked her in the eyes as I said my next words. *"When did you decide to keep your male?"*

Kassie's lips parted, eyes widening in shock.

201

I was just as stunned by my own words as well. It wasn't something I ever expected to say. Hell, after Helen, I didn't think I'd ever want to keep anyone again—male or female.

But when that slut put her hands on Fin…

He was *mine*.

"If you're asking me that…" Kassie exhaled, her voice trembling. *"Then you've already made your choice. It was too late for me to walk away after the first time I had him."*

"Then I'll keep him."

The words came easy now.

Kassie had just helped me make a decision I hadn't even realized I was wrestling with. *Adapt or die*—I'd learned that a long time ago. And right now? I was adapting.

"Theia is *never* going to believe this when we get her back." Kassie gave me a wary smile.

"She'll get over it, or I'll punch her in the face." I began to move toward the kitchen but hesitated. "What does this mean for us?"

Her brows knotted in confusion. "What do you mean?"

"For twelve thousand years, it's been just us—me, you, and Theia. Now you and I have males."

"It means you knock before barging into someone's bedroom," Clay called from the kitchen.

I turned to find him standing beside Fin—who was watching me with a small, satisfied smirk.

My jaw clenched. "It's going to take some time before I get used to you speaking to me, Swamp Ape."

Clay shrugged. "Kassie, tell your sister she's now my sister, and I'll gladly take her verbal abuse if it makes you happy."

202

"I want to kiss you, but I'm still worried you'll rip my arm off or something," Fin admitted, his expression torn between hesitation and need. "Even if you did just declare you're keeping me."

"Fucking males." I rolled my eyes as I walked into the kitchen, intending to get a cup of coffee.

"Here." Fin was already waiting, holding out a mug of black heaven. "Does this make me a *good* male?"

I took the cup and held eye contact with him as I took a sip from the steaming mug before responding. "This morning made you a good male. This makes the world tolerable."

He shook his head, still smiling. "You have no shame, do you?"

"When you've been publicly beaten and raped for entertainment, you learn that shame means nothing." I didn't lace my words with poison. Just cold, simple truth. Fin's smile vanished, his face paling as horror settled into his features.

"Shit," Clay said, his face set in shock.

I shrugged. "We fixed it a long time ago."

"Ella—" Fin's voice cracked, barely above a whisper.

"Don't," I said, my voice firm. "I was only explaining why shame has no place in my life." I turned to Clay. "I have good reason to hate males."

"Ella, our males aren't them," Kassie said simply, stepping up to Clay and slipping an arm around his waist.

"I didn't say they were," I replied, my tone sharp but controlled. "I'm going to enjoy my coffee now while Fin looks for leads."

203

I walked out of the kitchen and sat on the couch, waiting for Fin to follow. When he entered, I pointedly looked at the seat next to me, then at him. "Teach me, and after we find Theia, we will find Ares."

"Ares?" Fin sat down beside me, opening the laptop. He glanced at me, his brow furrowed in confusion.

"So we can kill him."

He turned fully to face me, his eyes wide. "You want to kill the GOD OF WAR?" He stressed the title as though it should mean something to me.

"That's not a bad idea." Kassie's voice came from the doorway as she and Clay walked in. "We get Theia back, lure Daddy Dearest into the swamp, and the five of us take his head."

"Why do the two of you want to kill your father so badly?" Clay asked, sitting in a chair and pulling Kassie onto his lap.

I tilted my head and met his gaze. "He deserves it."

"Good enough for me." Fin shrugged, then turned back to the laptop. "But your missing sister is a priority." He started explaining what he was doing as he began searching, his voice lowering as his focus shifted to the task at hand.

Chapter 19

Ella...

By the time the sun set, Kassie and Clay had gone to bed, and Fin and I set out to check the local bars rumored to be connected to the black market. We turned down an alley that wasn't really an alley at all. It would seem like a dead end to humans, but immortals knew better—it led to an underground parking garage.

Fin parked the truck and glanced at me. "Let's focus on finding the weeping water. It's gotta be more specific than just getting water from the creek."

I rolled my eyes. "You said that last night. Let's just see what we can find."

"Try not to start any fights this time." He flashed me a smile as we walked around the truck.

"If I choose to have a little fun while looking for my sister, I'm allowed."

He arched an eyebrow, a hint of amusement in his gaze. "You do realize it makes it harder for us to find leads that way, right?"

205

I shrugged, not particularly bothered by the risk. As we walked into the building, the dim light of Edison-style bulbs illuminated the space, casting a buttery yellow glow that reminded me of a speakeasy.

"I make no promises."

As usual, Fin and I split up, once we entered the bar, each of us searching for leads. The leather-padded seats and the dim light, which glinted off the amber liquid in the bottles, only added to the atmosphere. It was the perfect place for shady dealings. My sister would thrive in a place like this—just like she had when mortal speakeasies started popping up all over.

It didn't take long for Fin to find me. He'd uncovered the lead I couldn't. If I was being honest, I wasn't cut out for this kind of thing. Fin could approach anyone and knew exactly what to say. Communication wasn't my strong suit.

"What did you find?" I asked.

"I learned the legend of the Weeping Waters has a dark side that mortals don't know about. The grief of those tribes became a living thing—a creature that resides in the water itself. If I had to guess, I'd say that creature holds the key to getting those vials."

"Are we looking for this creature, then? If we are, what did you find out about it?" I was already heading for the door. We'd obtained the lead, and the bar had outlived its usefulness.

"It has no known weaknesses. It's said to have dragged immortals to the bottom of the lakes, leaving them broken-hearted in its depths. Some immortals have been retrieved, but they've never fully recovered. They're said to live with a permanent chill.

206

It's just called the Creature of Weeping Water." Fin followed me, explaining what he'd learned.

"So this creature breaks hearts and leaves immortals to drown for all eternity—unless someone pulls them back to the surface. Somehow, I relate to that."

For most of my life, all I wanted was to set the world on fire and watch it burn—for my pain and my sisters' pain.

"You don't have to drown any longer," Fin said, his eyes filled with pain as he looked at me.

"You are such a girl. Let's get going." I didn't want to linger in that moment. "I'll text Kassie what we found." I pulled out my phone and climbed into the truck.

"I'm going to drive to the lake and use my phone's hotspot to try hacking into the cameras around there. See if I can spot them," Fin explained as we pulled out of the underground parking lot, heading toward Nebraska and leaving Kansas behind.

***

Ella...

Three hours later, we parked at an overlook beside a stream that flowed into the dark, haunted body of water. Fin got out of the truck and opened the back door, rummaging through his bag to pull out his laptop. We might have started an actual relationship, but he was still all business, and I liked that. I was beginning to admit there were things I'd liked about him all along.

I climbed out, tugging on my jacket against the chill of the night air. "I'm going to walk around a bit and check things out."

207

"Do me a favor and stay where I can see you," he said with a half-hearted smile. "If shit goes down, I don't want to miss out on the fun." I knew what he was really doing—trying to protect me without making it obvious. Part of me was irritated by it, but the other part… was touched.

I thought back to how Theia had been taken because we were separated. "I know better than to go into the unknown alone. That's how Theia got taken." With that, I began to walk around, my eyes scanning the darkness. I paused in several spots, constantly scanning the water's edge. What were the chances they hadn't made it here yet? Finally, I reached the edge of the stream that fed into one of the man-made lakes.

"I know that sssmell," a gurgling voice called from the dark water just a few feet away.

My head jerked toward the water, and my body tensed, ready for a fight. "Show yourself."

"You are not the sssad Sssiren from before. Do you have sssorrow?" The creature's voice slithered from the water.

"You mean Theia?" I asked, my stance still tense. Had this thing done something to her?

"Sssuch anger. They had anger; their anger led to the tearsss that created me." The creature continued speaking, remaining hidden in the dark water.

"You are the Creature of Weeping Water?" I asked, my mind racing to gather any clue about my sister.

"Yess. Do you have sssorrow to feed me or just your sssisster?"

"What did you do to my sister?" I demanded, the edge of my voice sharper now.

208

"She had her own ssssorrow. Sssorrow sso deep. I tasted her tearsss and washed them away. She left with her sssweet sssorrow." There was a tone of regret in the creature's voice.

"How long ago did she leave with her sorrow?" I pressed, hoping to get something—anything—about Theia. I knew my sister had sorrow. Sorrow was what she and Kassie shared, though the source of their pain was different.

"Ssstep into the water and I'll tell you."

"Can my anger feed you?" I countered, the words sharp. Fin had shared what he'd learned about this creature, but this one wasn't in the lake—it was in the creek.

"I can give you sssome of my sssorrow," the creature offered, its strange voice almost pulling me forward, tempting me to step into the dark water.

"I don't need your sorrow. I need my sister." I turned and began walking back toward the truck. No way in hell was I going to be trapped in endless sorrow, not when I had my own problems to handle.

"Wait!" the creature called out from behind me, desperation in its haunting voice.

In the darkness, I saw Fin's head jerk in my direction. He'd heard it. I glanced back at the water. "I only want my sister. If you can't help me, then my anger and I are leaving."

"How much blood have you ssspilled? How much sssorrow have you caused?" It shifted tactics, no longer seducing me with sorrow—it was using guilt now.

"As much as I've been given," I replied flatly. Guilt had no place here. I needed to find Theia, and nothing would distract me from that.

209

"Angelica did that. Her sssorrow burned ssso hot, there were no tearsss for me." The sound of sloshing water made me tilt my head and narrow my eyes, trying to spot the creature hiding beneath the surface.

"Angelica?" I asked, my voice edged with confusion. Was the creature talking about someone other than Theia?

"She is new to our world. The watersss speak; they carried her ssstory to me. Your sssister came daysss ago."

"Thank you." I wasn't sure if the creature's words were a gift or a warning, but I didn't have time to think about it. Theia had been here. That was all that mattered.

"And your Vampire friend? Doesss he have sssorrow to give?" Water sloshed, and something surged from the depths—a shifting mass of darkness, half-shadow, half-liquid. Human hands clawed at the ground, but its mouth was wide and fish-like, lips too thin, its face featureless except for sunken indentations where eyes should have been.

"Not tonight, Creature." I turned, ignoring its protests from the water as I closed the distance between Fin and me, grabbed his arm, and pulled him away. "It's hungry. I'd stay back."

I didn't want to admit how tempting it had been to step into the icy water when it had beckoned me. Its strange, gurgling voice had almost pulled me in, but I could guess—based on the feeling in my bones—that it had some sort of persuasive ability. Maybe it was because we were Sirens, daughters of a God, that my sisters and I were resistant to such powers. Vampires, though, didn't have that luxury.

210

"Is that the Creature of Weeping Water?" Fin asked, walking with me back to the truck.

"Yes, it said Theia was here days ago. Apparently, it fed on some of my sister's sorrow. I don't know if that's a good thing or not." Worry for my sister clawed at me in tandem with the crunch of gravel under my feet.

"Shit. I'll pull up footage of this area from two days ago and start from there."

"What's next on the list?" I asked, my thoughts still scattered, searching for any thread to hold onto. We were still behind. All our efforts to catch up—or even to get ahead—had brought us right back to square one.

"There isn't anywhere in the state to get the feather. There was a place in Texas, from what my contacts said, but I don't see them backtracking for that. We should probably head north. You drive; I'll put in the location of the next safehouse on the GPS and search the cameras as long as my signal holds." We climbed into the truck, and as I texted Kassie the address Fin had entered, I couldn't shake the feeling that we were chasing ghosts, always one step behind. But we had no choice but to keep moving.

211

Chapter 20

Ella...

We reached the safehouse an hour before dark. Fin had lost signal along the way and hadn't been able to find any leads.

"You keep looking for leads. I'm going to the store to grab something for dinner. Don't expect anything fancy—it'll probably be frozen pizza or something." Theia would hate frozen pizza. She actually enjoyed cooking. Me? I never saw the point in learning more than the basics.

Fin glanced out the window. "I'd go with you, but I'm not sure we'd make it back before sunrise."

"I can just order delivery again," I offered, not wanting to be separated from him. It was strange, even after everything.

"That works for me." He patted the seat beside him. "I can keep teaching you if you want."

I sat next to him. Once I'd finished ordering food, he began explaining what he was doing and how. I didn't understand any of it, but hearing him talk was nice somehow. I didn't understand what was happening to me. If I were one of my sisters, I'd talk about it, but I wasn't them.

By the time the food arrived, the sky had already started to lighten.

Sometime after we'd finished eating, Fin found an image of the Jeep we were looking for. Unfortunately, that glimpse was all there was. The fucking Lycan was good at staying off the cameras. At least we had confirmation—they had been in Weeping Water, Nebraska, three days ago, not two.

Hours passed, and I leaned my head on Fin's shoulder as he typed, frustration building with every dead end. He froze at the contact and looked at me.

"Is this not okay?" I asked, staying still.

"I just wasn't expecting it."

"You make me… feel things," I admitted. "I've never felt comfortable with a male before. I'm trying."

"We are immortal. While I want this—you close to me—we have all the time you need." His head tilted, resting lightly against mine as he reassured me, something I hadn't realized I needed. Was this what Kassie felt with Clay? This need, this comfort?

"I'm going to bed, and I want you to help me sleep. You have my permission to touch me." The admission wasn't easy, but it wasn't as hard as I'd thought it would be either.

With that, I stood, grabbing my bag from the living room before making my way to the bedroom he'd claimed. Was this how Kassie felt? Was this what she did? Was I doing this right? I hated males, and yet… I needed this one. I needed Fin. Adapt or die. This was an adaptation I wasn't sure I minded making.

Fin followed, closing the door behind him. "How do you want me to help you sleep? You're in control here—always."

213

"Strip and sit on the bed," I commanded, pulling my shirt over my head and pushing my pants down my legs. Left in nothing but a black bra and panties, I stood before him, letting him look. His throat bobbed as his gaze roamed over me, but I wanted more—I wanted his hands. Yet I knew he wouldn't touch me unless I told him to, and somehow, that made heat pool between my legs. A strange hum curled in my throat, something I'd never felt before—almost like a purr.

He stripped and sat at the edge of the bed, completely bare. I unhooked my bra as I approached, watching how his eyes tracked my every movement. I let it slip to the floor, then bent at the waist, stepping out of my panties—slow and deliberate. And still, he didn't move. The power that surged through me, knowing I had this control over him without using my ability—*fuck*.

"The last time a male was behind me, I felt only pain," I said as I straddled his lap. Was I ready for him to erase that? Could I let him take me like that without reacting with the violence I'd been honed for? There was a war waging inside of me—wanting him to take it from me but wanting him to only do what he was told. I wanted him to erase every male that had ever touched me, even if I was afraid.

"Then allow me to show you how it should feel."

He moved with a fluid decisiveness, rolling me onto my stomach, any former hesitation gone. A slow drag of his hands traced a path over my skin, beginning at my hips, moving up my stomach, over the curves of my breasts, until he settled at the sensitive hollow of my throat. His fingers curled, angling my chin up, his fangs grazing my skin, sharp and deliberate. Shivers ran

214

down my spine as his warmth bled into me, his chest pressed firm against my back, his erection teasing against me.

"Tell me what you want," he murmured. "Do you want me buried inside you? My teeth and my cock? Do you want me to make you cum in every position?" His grip tightened ever so slightly, his breath a brand against my ear. "I won't do it unless you tell me to."

He was still asking permission—even now—when I knew how badly he must want just to take me. "Yes," I breathed.

"Yes, what?" His voice dripped with amusement as he kissed my neck, teasing the head of his erection against me—but barely.

"Yes, Leech," I nearly snarled, pushing my hips back into him, forcing him just a fraction deeper.

He chuckled darkly. "I like it when you call me names." Then his hips snapped forward, and his teeth sank into my throat.

A sharp gasp tore from my lips, my eyes fluttering shut as pleasure bloomed through me. His tongue slipped over my throat as he moved inside me. His cock hitting a spot deep within that sent white-hot sparks racing up my spine. My body coiled tighter and tighter, wound like a spring as he took me from behind, his rhythm unrelenting, his touch burning into my skin.

His fangs withdrew, replaced by the slow drag of his tongue over the fresh wound. "Stretch your arms over your head, rest your chest on the bed," he murmured against my ear. "Trust me."

I obeyed, trusting him like I'd never trusted anyone before, needing the pleasure he brought me like I needed oxygen to breathe. My back arched, my ass clenched in his grip as he

215

drove into me, each thrust sending me closer to the edge. The angle—*fuck*. He knew exactly what he was doing, his cock hitting so deep it blurred the line between pleasure and pain.

"Cum for me, Ella," he huffed, his pace relentless, his voice raw with need.

And Gods help me—I did.

A choked sound tore from my lips as I came apart, tremors quaking through my body. My toes curled, my fingers fisted in the sheets, and my forehead pressed into the mattress as the orgasm crashed over me—relentless, unyielding. Wave after wave of pleasure wracked me, and still, Fin moved, thrusting through it, drawing it out, his own release still just out of reach.

"Fin!" His name ripped from my throat, pleasure cresting into something nearly unbearable as blackness burst into stars behind my eyes. Then his hips locked against mine, a guttural sound escaping him as he jerked, his release spilling deep inside me.

He stayed behind me, his hands smoothing over my shivering skin, grounding me as aftershocks rippled through my limbs. "That's how it's supposed to feel," he murmured, his breathing labored as his fingers traced lazy circles against my waist. "Do I need to show you again?"

I slipped my hand beneath me, my fingertips grazing his testicles. He twitched in response, his breath catching—just slightly.

I chuckled. *I fucking chuckled.*

"You are a cruel female," he said, his voice thick with amusement as he slid out of me and rolled onto his back. His gaze

216

was soft, his lips curved in a genuine smile. "Will you let me hold you?"

I hesitated. Then, slowly, I stretched out and scooted closer, allowing him to pull me into his arms. His warmth wrapped around me, solid and steady, his heartbeat thrumming beneath my cheek.

"I thought you were going to show me again," I murmured, a small, unfamiliar smile tugging at my lips. *Gods, when was the last time I smiled?* Laughter, lightness—I'd been without them for so long. And yet, somehow, he'd brought them back. *How?*

He chuckled, his fingers idly stroking my spine. "Whatever you want, I'll do it."

I pressed my cheek against his chest, listening to the steady rhythm of his breathing. "Erase them." My voice was quiet, almost lost in the hush of the room. Then I lifted my gaze, meeting his eyes. "Erase everything they did to me. Replace it all with you, with this—with what you do to me." A deep breath. "And when the sun goes down, we'll search for Theia. But until then…" My fingers curled against his chest. "Erase them."

217

Epilogue

Fin...

We had been traveling for weeks, chasing leads that led nowhere. The Jeep we'd been tracking on traffic cameras had taken us as far as Illinois—only to discover we'd been duped. The Lycan had hired a decoy, sending us on a wild chase while he vanished without a trace. We'd lost so much ground. Worse, we no longer knew what kind of vehicle they were even in.

For whatever reason, though, Nia had texted Ella and told her Theia was in Washington State. It was a mystery to me how the Priestess had known how to contact Ella or where her sister was. But at this point, we had no choice but to trust it.

Kassie and Clay were resting at our latest safehouse while Ella and I drove through the snow. There was a Shifter bar not far from here, one that might offer leads.

Weeks had passed since that first night. Ella had changed. Not much—but enough. She still stiffened when I reached for her sometimes, but she wasn't always angry anymore. In the quiet hours we spent tangled in bed, she'd let me in—little by little—offering fragments of her past. But out here, on the hunt, she was the same cold, distant female I'd met that night in Louisiana.

218

I glanced at her now, snow reflecting off her sharp features.

Was she disappointed in me?

I'd wasted weeks following that decoy. Had I let her down? Would she tell me when the sun came up? We hadn't spoken about it yet. Ella wasn't one to let things slide. She was direct—unforgivingly so. And from the start, she'd made it clear: *her sisters were everything.*

"Look out!" she yelled, pointing at the road as a figure darted out in front of us. I swerved and hit the brakes, going off into the ditch, the shock jarring our bodies.

Dear reader,

Thank you for reading! I intend to have the next book out as soon as possible. If you enjoy indie authors like me, check out www.indiebackbooks.com for indie author spotlights and other books! You can find all of my titles under the Paranormal Romance section of the site as well as links to purchase swag such as signed copies. You can also find my books, the first chapter of each, and upcoming releases by visiting www.authorruthnalio.com.

Book 4 blurb:

Male or female, it doesn't matter. They are all monsters. 12,000 years have done little more than confirm that over and over again. Theia continues living only for her sisters, hunting and destroying Ares, and for the soul she holds in her palm. When Kassie is taken by Bigfoot, Theia and Ella put hunting Aries on hold to track down the Swamp Ape. Theia soon realizes that splitting up to search was a mistake and finds herself surrounded by Lycans who want them all dead. Will this be her end? Will she finally be reunited with the soul in her palm? Or is this just a new battle to be fought on their endless quest to kill Ares?